i hope this

i hope this finds you

to the ones that could never belong

samica mehta

Notion Press

Old No. 38, New No. 6
McNichols Road, Chetpet
Chennai - 600 031

First Published by Notion Press 2017
Copyright © Samica Mehta 2017
All Rights Reserved.

ISBN 978-1-946822-97-0

This book has been published with all reasonable efforts taken to make the material error-free after the consent of the author. No part of this book shall be used, reproduced in any manner whatsoever without written permission from the author, except in the case of brief quotations embodied in critical articles and reviews.

The Author of this book is solely responsible and liable for its content including but not limited to the views, representations, descriptions, statements, information, opinions and references ["Content"]. The Content of this book shall not constitute or be construed or deemed to reflect the opinion or expression of the Publisher or Editor. Neither the Publisher nor Editor endorse or approve the Content of this book or guarantee the reliability, accuracy or completeness of the Content published herein and do not make any representations or warranties of any kind, express or implied, including but not limited to the implied warranties of merchantability, fitness for a particular purpose. The Publisher and Editor shall not be liable whatsoever for any errors, omissions, whether such errors or omissions result from negligence, accident, or any other cause or claims for loss or damages of any kind, including without limitation, indirect or consequential loss or damage arising out of use, inability to use, or about the reliability, accuracy or sufficiency of the information contained in this book.

Samica is not my biological daughter but our association is as old as she is. And its a matter of pride for me that even at this raw age she is showing signs of a genius. Her creativity and her passion for art are immense.

Her skills as a dancer are a treat to watch thus her admission for BA Honours Dance studies at University of Surrey, Guildford, UK did not come as a surprise.

She is a gifted writer as well. Reading through her articles one finds all the shades of life. There is that typical confused and insecure youth on one side, whereas you come across a passionate yet mature head on the other, and an old experienced octogenarian on a totally different tangent.

That is the beauty of her articles and that is the beauty of her personality as well. A near perfect package of a dancer, writer, sketcher, rolled into one.

'You are my master story teller', i often tell her, and not without conviction.

Be it the bright yellow, the bleeding crimson, the dull grey or the pitch dark, this girl knows how to create it and present it.

She is your girl next door who along with fighting out the typical trauma and challenges of teenage, ensures that she enjoys every moment to the hilt.

Keep it going Sam!

– Rakesh Gulati

*Letters from the series of
"Letters I never sent"*

hey,

i hope you're doing well

on all kind of days it is still going to be you, as silly as it may sound in today's times, which is filled with texts and Facebook and other numerous unfiltered communication arenas,

but sometimes i still sit down at my old rusty brown desk, with the old computer and the same old keypad i'm so used to, and write you ever lasting letters - about the things i would like to tell you, about my graduation and my internship, and my not so perfect sex life, about the fact that i almost burnt down my kitchen trying to cook,

and even about the new couch i bought.

its burgundy. you secretly always loved burgundy.

i'm sorry it took me so long to figure out.

hey,

i wondered.

i wondered today — what do the letters that you write but never post really mean?

and then i think of words like denial and oblivious and coward.

denial because these are feelings i don't accept. oblivious because i write these letters thinking i've let it all out and it has somehow just reached the idea of you, and that soothes my heart a bit.

and coward because i never post them, and i don't even intend to.

these letters help me cheat my heart. thats all there is.

its a cheat.

hey,

    i felt far today. far away from you.

    it feels like its been ages because i haven't seen you for a zillion seconds, but then it feels like it was just yesterday you walked away, because the wound still feels so cut raw and fresh, like i had just been bitten

    i look for marks on my body but don't find any and i don't know where the pain comes from

    it looks like its here to stay

    good laugh

    i want to confess

    that it scares me.

hey,

    its 2 am and i can't sleep

    i've started going to a therapist

    i still write because i never tried to forget you. you're anything but kind, loving, and gentle.

    and when i fell in love with you in a lucky summer of 2008, with a new scent of fresh university life and an adrenaline level as high as sky rockets, i prepared myself for the good and the bad. i prepared myself for this crazy ride our relationship was gonna be. cause it just wasn't normal, and out of everyone i guess you know what i mean.

    when i tell my therapist that our relationship was different and you became kinda addictive for me, she says its all a matter of time, and the addiction will go.

    its been 7 years.

hey,

i hope you're doing well

i turned 25 a few months ago, i was in Paris with my mom - and i think i saw you.

it was around 8 in the morning and you were standing near a river, with a steaming cup of espresso (extra cream, still.) your back was facing me and i don't know if i'm thankful for that, but i guess i am.

the high end point of your ears and nose were pink as a cake and you were vigorously typing out on your phone. and i just stood there with my jaw slacked to the ground because you looked like a man.

but you were still wonderfully just so you. your eyebrows weren't bushy anymore and your hair was still a mess, you wore this black metalled leather jacket which i think you wore more for the look of it, and brown gum boots. you looked good.

you looked - *you looked like a piece of me i would never get to touch, sense or kiss.* even from 30 feet apart i could smell the coffee and the cigarettes and just, you.

i wanted to cry.

my knees kind of gave out when you turned and swung your eyes searching for someone. and there was a moment when you planted your eyes at me, but that was for even less than a second and soon you were looking at other people. you didn't recognise me.

i got lost in the crowd.

i was one of the people,

but i'm glad. *i'm glad because i turned 25 that day and i got to see you.*

and i'm glad because i turned 25 that day and i got to be lost, finally, lost in one of your crowds - i got to be not seen.

and i got to lock myself with a pair of way too familiar brown eyes that have just somehow turned even a more beautiful shade of brown.

hey,

sometimes i'm all too tempted to call you and ask you how did you do it? how did you move on and how did you forget it all? but i still wish you luck, i still wish you all the happiness in the world, i still wish and pray the absolute best for you,

because beyond all the pain and the heartbreak and the unfixable cracks, you gave me the absolute best 3 years of my life, where you healed me and allowed me to heal you, where you taught that being irrational is completely rational, where every now and then you snuck out with me and we'd go to the nearest tattoo parlour to subside the ink kink we have. i really, genuinely, hope the best for you.

you were just something else.

fuck you though.

hey,

sometimes i still dream of things. and the worst part is those things aren't related to you or us, but they still remind me of pain, and pain reminds me of you.

handkerchiefs and burgundy couches, lamps with tea stains and light blue ink pots. these are the things you have no relation to. but maybe i stole a handkerchief from your collection every time i did laundry and i saw the way you looked at the burgundy couch when you chose a yellow, and lamps with tea stains caused one of our break ups and,

and blue ink pots. you wrote a good morning letter every Sunday morning when you rushed off to the studio early, i'd wake up snatching a handkerchief from the laundry basket, thinking of buying you the burgundy couch and smudging the tea stains on the lamp, and i'd look at that small piece of paper beautified with your fingers dipped in ink and *it would become another another extraordinary beat of my heart.*

hey,

i want to tell you a secret today.

with you everything was too much, when i hurt, i hurt so much so i preferred punching myself in the gut and knocking myself out for a couple of days. it was altogether a different species of love that not everyone gets, its toxic and addictive but at the same time its soft feathers and a bed of warm cotton. and even now, i don't know - *i don't know who intoxicated who.*

hey,

    its christmas

    i can see my neighbours slipping into duvets

    vanishing into another world through their off white curtains because its christmas.

    its christmas

    and you're not here.

    still, love

    i still wish you a galaxy of stars

hey,

    i stole

    i stole today.

i stole from my grandmothers' cupboard, a jar of raspberry jam. fresh and gooey. it melted on my fingers and my eyes watered. *it looked like the shade of your tongue.*

hey,

    i went shopping today.

    do you remember dreamcatchers?

    you used to scoff at them.

    but i saw you.

    i saw you when on rough nights with pieces of glass shattered on the floor because of my anger and me crumbled in a corner crying on the damage, you flicked the dream catcher, as if asking for magic, i saw your eyes and the way they looked at the feathers and the beads. i'm sorry i never told you this before.

    but i always

    always saw you.

hey,

    i remember your sayings about self hate

    someone called me an idiot today and i feel unwanted. at that hour i looked at the clock and it was dinner time, like that time we sat at the table eating mac and cheese with you holding my fingers, and whispering that self hate is something you can never escape because it doesn't know a goodbye.

    maybe you were right.

hey,

    i hope you're doing well

    its my mom's birthday today and she asked me about you.

    i looked at her and i remember,

    i remember forgetting how to speak.

hey,

    i hope you're doing well

    you're the reason behind brown sugars and brown breads. i so badly want the white. the white cubes of sugar and the white soft of bread but i got used to you and you got me used to the brown and its like i'll never see the bright of my life again.

hey,

    i turned 30 today and this is scary. ageing is scary. i see a little bit of grey ahead but no one to share it with,

    but what if i refuse to see the grey without you?

    what if i'm thinking of full stops?

hey,

stillness, do you know what its like to live in that?

do you know what its like to sip a cup of coffee that never feels warm and have a chilled drink that burns like lava? do you know what its like to touch but not feel and love with a heart that doesn't beat?

do you know what its like?

hey,

i love you, but i hope you enter 2017 in the company of another beating heart

i hope tonight you have someone to hold your hand

hey,

things have changed. its been 14 years, but i have a feeling that somewhere in this world you're sitting in the quiet corner of the library, still smelling of cigars and sunshines, having coffee and doing those silent sensual gulps that you always, always did.

you're away

but my eyes can't stop looking

at

for

you

hey,

    i have to tell you another secret today

    your name

    its not my favourite word anymore.

hey,

    i can't believe its been 15 years and i still write on my old desk.

    i want to share another secret with you today

    you know there are moments? moments where you're sipping something warm and sitting near the window with water dripping down the glass and you feel good and full about life even though you have a broken heart, you feel like you can make it and you don't think of full stops anymore.

    i had that moment today.

    i confessed to my therapist today that i don't think of full stops anymore and this is the last letter i shall ever write to the idea of you.

    you're kind, gentle, and all the amazing things in the world.

    but still, fuck you

My Vision

Addiction to Dusky Papers

those carved printed stories on paper saved me. in all kinds of ways. it saved me in ways one cannot 'practically' be saved. it saved me in ways my parents, friends or psychologist couldn't ever save me.

it made me clasp my hands for a moment to digest that overwhelming feeling of life drafted so gracefully on paper. making me realise how beautiful it is to have an alternate universe to escape into, or better, to just go to when you're having a hard time with reality.

that alternate universe gives me the strength i need to fight the harsh realities of life - the books i read taught me how actually everything in life is so much more bigger than what we think it is, that there's always a next page, a new chance or a new opportunity and if there's not a new page, you can always write it up, you can always create a new opportunity, you can always give yourself a second chance, you can choose to keep going no matter what happens, no matter how many paper cuts you get on your fingers.

the paper cuts. they show you kept going on - you kept reading because you're way too engrossed in living life, living the ups, the downs, creating experiences and drawing inspiration and strength from all the stories.

call me mad but when i go places, i unconsciously slip one of my favourite reads into my hand bag. knowing that its there gives me a certain unknown push or confidence to walk out of my comfort zone and face those faces, their words, the situations i'm put into. sometimes when i'm too scared, i take it out and open a random page, i look at the markings i've made, the words i've highlighted, the ones that had really got to me, and still do. i read them again, rather - whisper them to myself. a tinge of relief sweeps across my chest, i breathe out, slipping the book into my bag and slipping myself out into the reality. Just a few seconds of that alternate universe gives me hours of strength.

and i'm not sure if i'll ever be able to find a person who'd be capable of creating that kind of a magic for me.

people leave all the time any way. books don't.

Something Beyond Love

"you're my art," he said. and something inside her softened & slackened. she felt light. she just felt - light, always.

his paint brush & his lips simultaneously made contact with her skin. she could hear, see & feel him smile. all at once. that practically made her go insane. she closed her eyes. she stilled. not because she was scared, but because she wanted to enjoy this stillness with him.

stillness had always been an extremely big part of her life. she lived for those bare lifeless moments.

& if there's anyone she wishes to share it with - it's him. it's her stillness.

she won't share it with anyone and everyone. it's hers. but with him, she doesn't mind. she thought she would, but she realised she didn't. as his paint brush recklessly ponders over her cheek, down her collarbone, and her shoulder. all the smudged random paint making a beautiful mess out of her skin. he's not even kissing her anymore.

he's close but exactly an inch apart, almost intentionally. she could feel the heated & the cooled down rays of the sun sparking through the window & landing on them. almost reflecting upon their little perfect moment.

she inhaled the smell of this warm room. they spend more time here than their bedroom or kitchen or practically any other room in their house. this room was their little home. rays of sun sprawling across from the window, the light reflecting on his fingertips & his paint brush as he beautifully polishes down his tinted thoughts and in between moulds his brush with her skin as a surface instead of the white canvas itself.

she faintly opened her eyes & looked at his direction, his eyes were closed, smiling fondly at their memory from ages ago. he was feeling it, he still feels it - her stillness - their shared stillness. she almost felt her eyes inhaling his well sculpted face, now after all these years covered in beautiful lines and wrinkles, for the millionth time. and she could almost see the dazed patterns of colour surrounding the left side of her vision, she was covered in sprints of yellow, red, purple, blue, green, and all possible bright colours, for the millionth time.

she was the love of his life - and she was his art.

even after so many years she was surprised by how surprised she could still get by the warmth of this room, how light headed his paint brush makes her. they were so blessed. it's almost as if the kindliness of the tints of the sun rays and that paint brush uplifted the deterred broken cracks of their relationship when needed. and that's the exact difference between two people just being in love with each other and two people being in love with each other's soul and art.

something

something beyond love

Friends with misery

lets just be
> be friends
> *with your misery*
> *give your tears a little hug*
> *your lips a little kiss*
> *your sadness - a little hand*

5 Hours

there are your friends

then there are those people with whom you sit at 12 am in the night on your terrace with food and maybe a bottle of wine. you talk about stuff. you just talk.

you don't want advice and you don't need consolation. but you just talk.

because sometimes that's all you need to make things easier for yourself. you just need to talk to those people about how things have been, and what's going on with you. you just need them to listen. and they do. and surprisingly in those random 5 hours - *life gets better for you.*

I Think Its Lovely

its lovely

i think

its lovely to watch you sleep

with white sheets pooled near your ankles

your nightdress rolled all the way to your navel

bare clit and dirty scars from the whole day

your eye balls doing a little dance and your lashes changing colour

i think of the first day we met, *blue umbrellas and side street coffee shop smelling of wet sand, extra caramel leaking off your cup and the strap of your purple bra peeking off your work shirt*

i think of the first hug, me halfway leaning off my chair and you laughing off the awkwardness in my neck

its lovely

i think

its lovely to watch you sleep

the hair on your legs stand up bypassing chills and i'd wonder what you're thinking about

or when you take a deep sigh of relief and squeeze your legs tighter around my waist,

what is it that makes you sigh, or lay flat on your back with the elongated beauty of the swell of your breasts

its lovely

i think

that you're a deep sleeper

so sometimes i lay open mouthed kisses against your earlobe

or the creases of your forehead

the layer of sweat all pleasant against the flat of my tongue

"i think its nice that we can read together - my parents made love, cooked with their backs to each other, went to parties with stiff postures and uncomfortable clothes - the perfect ideal couple in the eyes of all, but my mother never sat with my father when he read his favourite self help books and my father never sat with my mother when she watched her favourite author talk on the television .

but i'm glad, i'm glad i can read with you, and watch television with you. i'm glad,"

its lovely

i think

its lovely when you're naked

i love you naked,

and i also love how you love yourself naked

i've seen people love themselves with the perfect dresses and perfect make up, perfect moods or perfect lucky days but when i just watch you stark naked - oh so bare - without a layer - at 3 am in the night making yourself a cup of hot chocolate, i just think, i just think

i just think its lovely

i look at the bundled skin between your thighs and the inviting dark bunch of curls right in between

i look at the creases between your armpits

and the sleepy bobbing of your throat

i kiss the space between your upper lip and your nose

feeling you stir slightly against the sheets, eyes scrunching and a yawn bubbling in your mouth

its 6 am - i think i should go to sleep

i close my eyes putting my most beautiful dream of watching you sleep to an end

i hold you, because i can, and let my body whisper

"you make self love look so easy and beautiful."

I can't

it doesn't really matter
    you get used to it
    you get used to watering yourself on your own
    pulling back the broken roots and wrapping them
    patting your chest where it aches a little
    sometimes
    sometimes staying strong is not enough
    sometimes you need a hand on your chest to remind you to breath in
    and a finger on edge of your knuckles to remind you to breathe out
    sometimes you need another pair of hands to hold you
    don't fight it
    sometimes
    you have to let yourself be held

Quiet strength

one day, it gets better

one day, i will wake up and getting out of bed won't be so hard

i won't feel like i'm paralysed

the small walk from my bed to the kitchen counter won't feel so heavy and my nostrils would welcome the cold breeze from the slightly ajar window

i won't panic about my chores or my work, or my relationship or my appearance

i'll wear the baggy denims without hesitation and i won't be ashamed of my unshaved arm pits

i'll put on the purple lipstick without a second thought and slip on my glasses without any doubt

i will tell my friend that i miss her without thinking that i'm unwanted

i will not question myself, i will not blame myself, i will not punish myself

i will live and let my mind live too

i'll take a deep breath when i'll feel the panic approaching and i'll draw soothing circles on my knuckles with my fingers to calm my pulse and heart rate

i'll smile at the person in the metro with the furrowed brows and tensed shoulders even though he won't smile back

i won't cringe or call myself names for tripping in front of my entire office and i won't physically hurt myself for not being promoted to the next position

i will call my mother first and tell her i miss her

i will have the energy and patience to ask about my sister's well being who doesn't even bother to call me anymore

and i believe if there's one thing that will never change will be the pain of abandonment, but i will welcome that too - i will feel the pain and embrace it openly but i will not fall weak

and when the clock will strike a dark digit like an 8, and people would leave to go home, i will slump my head down on the desk and wrap my arms around myself

a minute.

i will allow myself a minute to fall weak. to allow a tear to escape and my fingers to shiver as they want. just a single minute.

and i'll whisper to myself my most treasured secret,

"my quiet strength changes my world,"

because one day, it'll get better

Loving an Anxious Person

and it feels like the start of my favourite song

she can feel him vibrate against her in the bed. he's shivering even though the wind outside is warm and humid.

the room is dark and the moon outside does little to reflect his pale skin - pale, but a striking shining gold.

"*i really do try,*"

its a demeaning whisper that radiates so much of sadness that she feels scared of losing her own self and sanity in order to save him

but she lets him continue,

"*but i just can't get myself to want to wake up in the morning and face the things out there, my phone rings and i panic, someone touches me and i feel like someone's stabbing me. i can't help but feel useless, i can't even go to the grocery store without having 3 panic attacks in a row.*

i can't bring myself to show you the words i write or the books i love or the sonnets that make me think of you. sometimes… sometimes i even struggle to hug my own mom.

what does that make me? where am i? i cant breathe, i cant breathe at all, but God - please don't tell me to breathe, please don't tell me its okay that i can't buy my own coffee for myself. its like there's a heavy thread dangling from my body,

i'm on my way to a destination i know nothing about, after leaving a home that i didn't know was real.

what place is this?

it feels like the dead."

she shushes the trembling boy questioning his own existence, and luxuriates him with herself in her free versed thoughts and river of memories,

"*you know when i was 5,*

i got my first painting set by my brother, and i thought of drawing him first to show how thankful i was for his kind gesture, and when i gave him my first ever drawing, he laughed at me which felt a little unkind and thanked me, but the next day i saw the drawing crumbled in pieces on the top of the bin. and i thought what do you name people like that?

i still drew any way.

so when i was 9,

i decided to draw my mother. but i couldn't, i couldn't find the right angle of her face and her soft brows and her eyes that were my home. that made me cry, so she came to me and sat with me for 5 hours straight and helped me draw simple things like butterflies and roses and cupcakes."

she could feel his breathing evening out, although his anxious toes still danced the same, *"when i was 13,*

and got my first period during my school years, i got laughed at and bullied for having a couple red spots on my pants, and watched my own friends not willing to help me through it, i ran to the bathroom and cried for the next 2 hours, cursing myself and God for making me a girl and making me go through this, i childishly even cursed the colour red.

but later that night, for the very first time i got my first ever decent abstract piece, and i felt a tangle of pride i'd never felt before. the painting was all in red - dark red and light red and smudged red. and by the time i closed my eyes with the painting hugged tight to my chest, i'd firmly decided that my favourite colour will always be red,"

she could feel a silent smile on the nape of her neck,

"when i was 16,

i had my first kiss, just out of curiosity for wanting to know how it feels to have a pair of different lips pressed against my own. it was in a dirty cubicle of a dirty party with a dirty crowd i was trying to fit into, it tasted of smelling vodka and smoke and filthy words. i wish i'd saved my first for you, your shaky hands and your nervous sweating palms and your uneven pulse rate and your quivering hesitant lips,"

she could feel a silent laughter vibrating against her neck, and the pair of scared arms around her waist tightening,

"when I was 17,

and had sex for the first time, again out of curiosity, with an eager man with a lusted cock and rough hands. i limped for the next 3 days out of pain, and cringed for the next 3 weeks every time i undressed myself and saw the marks on my inner thighs and arms and hips that shouted pain and torture in the name of passion. and i again wished that i should have saved that first for you, for your nervous fumbling with the condom and the tripping over the duvets and soft promises and an undying passion that made me crave for more every single day,"

she could feel a breathy laugh that felt like relief against her neck, and if she noticed his tears sliding down her neck onto her collarbone, she didn't tell,

"and when i turned 18,

and started university, and met you, i tried so hard to befriend you. i read all the poetry books and novels i saw you carrying around the campus and reading in the library, but i swear, even till date i have no fucking clue as to who shakespeare is and what the fuck even made him so famous!

and then - then i got to see your scars and hear your stories about being bullied, i got to kiss your pain and share your anxiety and hug you when you whined with a heart racing at an untraceable beat. i got to know why your journal is so special to you, even more special than me.

i got to know about your favourite colour and snack, and i got to know about your dispassion for alcohol and public places and perfected people and this stereotyped circle of the society that you weren't a part of and didn't even want to be.

and i got to know about your depression.

i got to know about your anxiety, and how fucking real it is."

she pulls away and sees him smiling an unruly smile, a pure grin. she couldn't help but smile herself and pet him back to sleep, caress his arms and draw circles in the array of milk skin exposed between his briefs and his t-shirt, until he lulls into a deep sleep - only to be left with his crippling anxiety making a home under her own skin.

if she still thinks he needs a doctor, counselling, and a couple of pills to exist, rather than a struggling painter of a girlfriend and journals where he writes his anxiety and depression down, she doesn't tell him.

she loves him, she really does. but she still doesn't tell him how his first anxiety attack in front of her left her mentally shaken for months, left her with thoughts that barred her till date decisions.

she knows how he wants to wake up every day and get lost in the crowd, she knows and she can pin point the exact moments where she sees him scared, fearful, hesitant, and anxious, so damn anxious.

she's seen him struggle in the grocery store. she's seen him flinch by the smallest of touches even from his loved ones. she's seen him crying while he's deep asleep. she's seen him hole himself up in his journal and write all kinds of words with his dampened of a pen on paper, words that may not make him feel better,

but rather tell him that he does exist, that whats happening with him wont completely drown him for him to never return, the words tell him that the struggle is real, and the words a slight reminder that he's made it this far without giving up. he isn't emotionally dead yet.

she's seen it all, but she doesn't tell.

and even then when he's shivering against her hold in the small hotel room,

his fingers circling the lose threads and his toes tapping an anxious rhythm on the duvet in his sleep,

she doesn't point it out - his anxiety - but holds him a little degree tighter - *and it feels like the start of my favourite song.*

I Forgive You

you're you, still,

    and i'm?

    i'm i, still

    it's okay

    hush

    quieten

    don't whimper you foxy soul

    i forgive you

    it's aching a lot but i forgive you

    i will

    for all the kind smiles

    soft promising whispers

    melodious touches

    concerned frowns

    your anger and harsh palm dents imprinted across my cheek

    the breakdowns

thereafter

of apologies and brutally wounded love

the spilled pills across the bathroom floor

the flushed look of guilt hid behind your reflection in the mirror

with all the spots of undying blood plastered across our emotionally vacant flat

and for all the miserable tries of dragging something that had died during its first fumbled step

i forgive you - *i will forgive you*

just not now. not at this moment, but probably this same time, tomorrow,

i'll be not as much sore

my head will throb a little lesser and my heart will beat a little slower

after all the clock strikes the same time twice a day,

if my consciousness cannot, my unconsciousness will

has.

i forgive you, you foxy soul

i'll forgive you because i love you

so walk away

walk away

walk away before the broken pieces start to break more

and i

walk away

I Want to Choke on Self Love

it chokes

    the gulps, bites, scoops - even the gentle ones

    but who are you kidding?

    i don't know gentle

    i know gentle with my mom's hands, or my friend's heart

    but with me? my throat? my body?

    i don't know gentle with self

    i'm ashamed to feed off it,

    to like the burn, ache, or sting of it

    to wish upon stars of hardships for a permanent drown

    i'm ashamed i draw a flower,

    and it looks like a cage

    cage with feathered bars on the ceiling and sides and nail spikes for the floor,

    cage with walls full of blood written text,

dirty texts, confessions

"i'm not gentle with myself,"

i wish you'd love you

i'd put my nose to the red bloody text on the wall

high off the scent of metal

i'd put my tongue to the drop of blood sliding down

high off the taste of iron

metal and iron full of pain, full of unheard stories

loud with voices caged with flower petals

i'm ashamed - but i see a face,

there's a shine in her eyes and her torn plaided skirt twirls with happiness

her laughter bouncing off the bloody wall

it chokes,

the gulps, bites, scoops - even the gentle ones

i look at me, my expensive clothes and my too perfect make up

the fancy rings on my finger and a contact list to get more than lost in in my phone

i look at her

her torn skirt, her multi coloured socks and her rusty steel ring

that ring whispers, "i'm a priceless memory,"

and i wonder if the other sock belongs to her little brother i just look at her,

no, no

i look at her happiness

and i think - i want to kiss her

i want to kiss her laughter, her priceless memory of a ring and i want to wear her skirt and twirl with her

i want to stop choking on this taste of iron and metal

and stick flowers to this caged wall instead of bloody texts

i want to self love

i want to be gentle with myself

i want to place sunflowers in my palms and smile on softness

i want to self love

i want rusty rings for gifts and torn skirts to put my nose in and sniff life

i want to self love

i want to lick other reds - strawberry, cherry, carrot pies, roses

i want, i want.

i want to choke on self love

You

and then i thought its not okay

its not okay to sit in a circle of students in your class and feel wetness in your eyes

or to wonder and crave the magic of unconsciousness

to just not feel okay about the oxygen in your lungs

or for the day to come to an end

its not okay

hold me

internally

i want to be that hand you imagine on your scalp sometimes or your knuckles, or that small voice apologising for all the harsh things said or done to you, because no one deserves that.

i want to be the sugar you can't taste no matter how many spoons you pour, or the arm nudging you a step extra when you're about to back off because you need to know failure too.

i want to matter so much and at the same time not exist

and i'm sorry that some people don't look through,

that some people don't notice living at the peak of obliviousness,

some people don't realise your contemplating thoughts about the good your absence might bring or do.

no one should have to do it alone, eat lunches in bathroom cubicles or cry alone in the middle of a bright day in busy buildings - busy with education, people, friends, syllables, emotions, life? and a small bump of sobs in a corner.

i'm sorry you lost your safe space.

the sun is shining but isn't all that bright, and i see your tea is running cold. your lips look white and your eyes pour loneliness. you whisper, i remember the last beautiful thing i saw was my mother's laughter while cutting that burnt christmas apple pie.

"hey, you got this"

you wonder who said that

you look up from your half eaten sandwich, its side crumbs wet with your tears. the tiled wall stares back at you.

it was you.

its okay if this is what you are right now - someone who eats her lunches in a cubicle because this world is scary, and its okay if this is what you wish to be for a while, because you are your own human.

Movie Hall

do not give up - they all say, don't they?

    to keep looking, keep searching, keep risking, keep trying

    my spent mind asks how many more tries

    my spent body doesn't know the answer

    nor does my psychiatrist, or psychologist

    i hugged myself closer, tighter, firmer on the closed toilet lid

    realisation daunting in and out

    the feeling of my feet hanging off the edge of a building 3000 meters high

    the feeling of senses being numb

    smells smell-less

    things unseeable

    voices inaudible

    the choir of imaginable souls around you chants

    do not give up

    you stare at them for seconds

minutes

and then

then you laugh in their fucking face

a thing as normal and ordinary as a movie hall - unbearable.

and my brisk walks out of the hall, my desperate sprints

and i asked myself, how do you train yourself the normal skill of watching a movie in a movie theatre with your loved ones all over again?

how do you get used to a movie hall again?

how do you not puke at the smell of delicious food again?

i can't remember.

its not complicated

they say

its simple - enjoying a movie at a movie hall

so simple

but do you wanna know a secret?

the word 'movie hall' shreds me to bits

so i did what i always do

i cried for an hour, exhausted myself enough for an extremely lulled and numbing sleep

heavy lids help - i husk to me

walk to the hall, putting in earphones with no music on

allowing a sense of safety

and i thought again to myself all sad - "earphones with no music on."

numbness, the next 2 and a half hours, numbness

but i'll tell you a secret

12 minutes, the first 12 of the movie i tried to watch,

the first 12 i allowed myself to see, to laugh, to enjoy

only,

my lips stayed shut as the whole hall laughed

my eyes brimmed up blurring my vision as the whole hall widened their eyes engrossed at the visual story

my breathing became erratic as the whole hall gasped to not laugh and breathe

my mouth went dry tasting like metal as the whole hall enjoyed corns and muffins

i tried.

and after 12 minutes of.. trying?

i turned around in the chair, made a ball of myself, a very small ball, a ball one wouldn't see if you walked past by me,

i slept blankly for 2 and a half hours in a hall full of slurps, laughs, fond snorts and happiness.

and for those 2 and a half hours i asked one basic thing - "how does it feel like to enjoy a movie at a movie hall?"

and i can't remember.

why am i even holding on anymore?

i can't remember.

i can remember one thing though,

i remember slices of warm pie, dollops of ice cream, warm meals, the way my mum would hum a beautiful tune around the house fixing meals and my favourite kind of tea,

my ballet shoes and my sister's erratic chirped calls of her first day as a doctor, my dad's unconditional strength and evergreen warmth,

i remember rains, dusts of sand and sunsets, and kitten licks of my dog across my check,

i remember it all - these dreams i entertain when i'm too close to jumping,

and now, i remember.

i remember why i'm still holding on.

I Stare and Walk Away

the sunflower faces a little north

   direction of this boy

   its raining

   can you smell the lilting sunflower?

   its yellow, facing down with drops of water sliding down the baby leaves on its stem

   there are insects coming out from where it grows on the ground, going in all norths and souths, some easts and some wests

   and i wonder

   i wonder how deep does the root go

   how deep would you have to dig to rip it out and kill the flower and destroy it

   making the bright yellow a dark brown reminding you of death

   of how i feel

   of trauma

   abuse

wounds

cuts

or maybe a small broken heart

i stand on the edge of the sidewalk, you're sat at the same table near the window head, maybe still loving the melody of sky and chymes of the door bell. your coffee still sits near your left hand. you're on your second cup, and i reckon one more is on the way.

i want to ask how you are but your smile talks so nice to me. like the corner of your lips recognise my existence and the moist forming on the window decides against all odds, reflecting the chill off your slick bland skin and,

and i'm dying here

the ink bleeding from your pen and the rough used edges of your journal tells me you've been good. you've been you.

i miss you, oh so much, but i still smile, for some loves - no matter how painful the memories or the heartbreak - will forever hold the endless power to make you smile.

its raining, i stare for another twenty seconds, and walk away.

the sunflower faces a little south

direction of this girl

its raining

can you smell the lilting sunflower?

the way it sways and dances its pain

the way its named after light but looks so sad

i reckon it misses its daisy

that is how i remember myself

on an old summer, years ago

with this boy looking like the jewel in the crown

the sunflower

i sit in this old cafe

reminiscing feelings like warm hard chest and brown back musty hair fading off to the line of a beautiful prick

loving the melody of sky and chymes of the door bell, my coffee sits near my left hand and one more is on the way

i look at the hollowness of the chair ahead of me

gasping hard to keep up the lies

i reckon i look like i'm doing so good

i hold the nib of the pen tighter

every time i feel a dab on my foot i look down the table, beside the chair, across the cafe, beyond the reality, and every time i see nothing. it doesn't hurt anymore but i still sniff our love and it's like i meet you for the first time all over again,

right here

just

like

right over here

i shave off your beard again, and cut your toe nails with care

your chest all bare, and a white warm tongue surfaced evenly on the slope of my neck watching you suck your thumb during thunderstorms and cut cucumbers all square shaped

the bell chimes and i look at the young boy walking in

eyes avoiding humans and music blasting his ears

lyrics along the lines of love sucks

and i want to go up to him so bad

so bad and tell him it doesn't, tell him about you - *your first winter hellos and goodbyes like a warm thermal in a snowstorm*

i smile

right here

just

like

right over here

i think some loves - no matter how painful the memories or the heartbreak - will forever hold the endless power to make you smile

and then i think you shouldn't let go off loves like that. you fight for it day and night.

you fight to be fought for.

my pen slides the end of the page

i look out the window, i see the sunflower hanging in between, as if it doesn't know where's south and where's north

i see more sunflowers

i see the side walk

i see nothing

i stare for another twenty seconds

and i keep staring

its been 2 hours

i'm still staring

its been another 2 hours

i never wanna stop staring

Couches and Lamps

couches and lamps and your silent reading glasses

   people don't like you? oh

   you're kinda somehow one of those very few

   well i know i'd die without the aura of your handmade coffee when i get back home, or my walk into the house would be incomplete without stumbling over your messy boots and shrugged wet jackets, or,

   the necklaces would dangle

   there's no silver but only metal

   no gold but only copper

   copper with a lot of rust on it

   you love old things

   you loved the second hand books i got you for valentine's day and you loved the old quill i got you because you said it reminds you of ageing and what a beautiful phenomenon that is

   it didn't make sense to me but you do

   but i still don't know why people don't like you

   we love holding each other

but you hate wearing heels

i asked you why

i probably shouldn't have

my heart couldn't stand being swollen with so much affection

you'd said you're too much used to the musky smell of my armpits and the way your temple fits against the depth of my chest, the way you love the fabric of all my shirts or the sensation of my skin against yours, you'd said you love the contrast our skins make, the beauty of indifference that it radiates,

i'd be reading the morning newspaper and you'd suddenly come and sit beside me, i won't bother because i know you. you'd take my palm and i still won't bother because i know you. you'd compare the tone of our skins for a good two minutes and i still won't bat my sight towards you. after a while you'd tuck your head in my neck as if the shades of our skin got you drunk. just like that.

because we love holding each other

it doesn't make sense but you do

i think i'm starting to know why people don't like you

i know you cry and you're one of those who hates being held in such moments

so i just watch you cry

and sometimes a hiccup would force you to look at me and id smile at you from where i'm stood in the doorway because i can, you won't smile back but you keep looking, and looking - as if there's nothing else that there is and i'm all you see - like i'm the darkness you crave in too much light - and that sense of sadness you need to feel human when things are too pretty perfect,

i know it doesn't make sense but you do
and i guess i know why people don;t like you
couches and lamps and your silent reading glasses
you'd tell me you'd walk on moons and id believe you
or that you'd inevitably break my heart some day
and i'd believe that too
i know now that people don't like you
it doesn't make sense but you do
they like loyal but not honest
they like love but not commitment
they like being looked at but not really seen
and you're not people

you're honesty and commitment and unwritten songs left abandoned in the studios for they reveal too much and you're that collection of ideas that's capable of changing the world but doesn't because

because people, honey
people are not worth it
it doesn't make sense but you do
couches and lamps and your silent reading glasses
i know why people don't like you
it doesn't make sense, but you do
you always do.

The Hands of an Artist

hands.

they are worn out and remind me of black.

blank and black. an unrecognisable mixture of experiences, colours, moods, and souls.

an inevitable result of mixing a bit of too much of everything. a beautiful experience of going over board with your creativity. open to interpretation of the soul and figure, eyes and nose, its lips and ears.

they smell of bland freshly brewed black coffee. a smell that stings my senses and warms me up just so right. the smell is as comforting as a non-verbal conversation between two souls. they smell of a cloth that's been used way too much - that just one more flick of touch and it might tear into bits and pieces of unfixable threads, but each thread having created so much that it overwhelms you and hurts your chest.

out of all the things and possible body contacts, i love this one of the most - holding his hand, interlocked fingers. its so intimate that i can't help but close my eyes and just inhale this intimacy. it makes me stronger, brighter, it charges me up like nothing else, an unnamed energy that feels too much like magic, and too much like love.

its got that familiar scent and faded shade of paint colours from earlier today, the chapped and bitten borders of his finger nails because creativity and anxiety go hand in hand, the wedding band on his ring finger inevitably making me a spiritual part of all of his creations and the drunken magic he pours on his canvas and papers and books and sheets.

the skin burn at the base of his wrist, its deep and years old, its a slender brown black line, the history behind that scar pulled the strings within me in an incurable way, filling me up with fondness, warmth, appreciation and unutterable respect for this man i'm insanely and irrevocably in love with.

just the press of his hand against my cheek is more than enough to stop the tears from sprinkling out. its warm and so soft that i can't help but always lean in, inhale the addictive smell and nudge my face, intending to go in impossibly closer and deeper. furthermore, the soft swift of his knuckles against the freckles near my eyes and the lines on my forehead, flattening and fading those lines with a promise to never return. the ache is still there in my chest but its soothing, like it knows its being taken care of, there's nothing to worry about and be anxious about. the moulding of his palm and my cheek shouts and screams - 'its all okay,' and with all the calmness in my body i believe it.

it took me long enough to realise his hands, his source of creation, of painting, of writing gives me life. and not just a life, more like a series of overwhelmingly perfect breaths. inhaling and exhaling unreachable amount of peace and happiness. driving me into this parallel universe of stillness, of his art and the addicting(addictive) rusty feel of his skin.

i can't help but close my eyes, leaning into his touch and sigh heavily in appreciation. i stay like that for god knows how long. it's been a long day of human interactions and pretentious conversations that don't settle in too well with me. i lose track of time and i guess so does he.

this is how i survive. *this is the cure i come home to.*

his hands.

worn out and black.

Prison Cell

prison cell isn't a place for love.

behind constricting bars that feel way too much like protection from the rest of the world and locked cells that give way too much emotional freedom to punished souls swaying heavily into one another.

the hours get lost in all kinds of clocks and day time isn't particularly day time anymore for it stops mattering,

as in the late hush of the night in the dull corner of the cell, with creaked walls and pole-shaped shadows sprawled in front of their feet, secrets are shared, soulful knowledge is filled in the emptiness and vulnerability is accepted. two figures accept each other for who they really are, despite one being a thief and other being a murderer.

a thief that steals for poor and a murderer that kills a rapist.

more secrets are shared, about favourite music and favourite books, about the happiest memory and the weakest moments. while one hesitantly whispers about the broken dreams of buying his mother his favourite car, the other confides about the wet tear stained faces of his family that haunt him every night. tasteless baked potatoes become groggily tasteful when shared over those secrets and the tearing wallpaper of the wall behind their backs form beautiful adored patterns on the floor.

life stories are relayed like fun riddles and incomplete pieces are silently filled by a gentle squeeze of two manly and sweaty palms that holler and scream coexistence and maybe something like love. invalid points are accepted and failures are laughed at. dreams are explored and boundaries are widened with growing hope and confidence from the reassuring glances of the other.

they share touches that feel tender and emotionally neurotic, loved countenance given for nasty scars and foul odour off their prison clothes, and the gazes — they gaze at each other with things that aren't entitled to them by human breed — with delicacy, and with some kind of worth.

and they laugh, they humorously bask in how many little fucks they give about the things and the populace that exists beyond the sheltered boundaries of this prison cell,

as two masculine body frames settle comfortably beside each other and against the hardness of the wall, abandoning the uninviting comfort of the bunk beds, breaths evening out in a sync and lulled into another unvoiced night of sharing something that feels like love in a place full of people abandoned and disregarded by the society,

bizarre and ironical,

love in a prison cell is somehow just thousand times brighter, truer, and purer than love in hoax bright colours of the doomed society.

Settling Anew

its like settling anew.

    with sugar brown boxes scattered across the room, ducked in tape and some half open. objects falling out. the whole scene reminds me of showers in a new bathroom for the first time, the hiss on your tongue when the cold water touches your back and teases you, the spilling of milk when you work the new coffee maker wrong and the forgetful count of the number of shelves in your new closet. the shoe you can't find and your favourite bowl has a crack now. its painful. the crack is painful. but you still have the bowl and its got nowhere to go. you're here to stay in your new little home. the couch looks a little out of place but that's okay, as long as it sinks in just right and the beautiful rays of the moon smile a little brighter than the suns, if compared to the previous home and you wonder why. maybe it's because of your strength. how many people have the strength to shift their roots but settle in with a smile?

you gave a face to my future and my dreams

you gave my path a direction

my calls of hope a voice to reach

my eyes a sight to see

and its like settling anew

To not Label

i tried with other people - but they responded in a manner that made me detest the human species and feel ashamed of being one.

'cause you know i got this one person — just this one person who knows how to soothe out my dark clouded thoughts, my false images of myself in the mirror, my shivers and my nervousness. that person's the reason why i have a built up self worth today. i cannot define myself without that person and i think that's kinda scary but equally okay.

there is this species of thoughts i can't put into words, or letters, or even actions. that frightens me. Because although it is extremely overwhelming to have such heavy thoughts within me, i need to get them out.

i need to communicate them.

its as soothing as the magical mixture of all the rainbow colours combined but as burning as nicotine for a non-smoker.

and this person - i share this dumb silence with, and have these conversations that go way beyond words and syllables. Its unknown, unsettled, unsure, unresolved, unnamed - but its the medicine that fills the cracks of my self worth and my too vulnerable emotional skin.

every Sunday evening when all the students from all the dorms go out and get themselves wasted and lost and drunk enough to forget everything, i go to this broken bench behind the boundaries of the football field. if someone else came here, they'd probably shout and leave, calling it scary and haunting.

but for me really its the addictive calm this place carries and offers me. its got its own high to it. and that person kinda makes it even more special.

this broken wooden bench which shouldn't be as comfortable as it really feels, and the familiar creek sound it makes when i sit on it, making me realise that i actually do miss this sound the whole week. i hold my sketch book in my hand and my pencil, just in case inspiration decided to kick in. i think one of the main reasons i'm drawn to this place and this person is because I'm constantly looking for inspiration, and constantly looking to create.

he usually shows up within the gap of 10-20 minutes, with a cigarette dangling in between his long fingers. i have a weird fetish for his hands, and the chapped skin around his nails that he plucks when he's nervous, i reckon.

his facial features not extremely familiar because i've never really seen his face in daylight, ever - but there's this shape and this odd sense of space that his facial features carry and fill that seems familiar, that i'd recognise this figure in dark in less than a second. the clothes on his figure almost always hang loosely and rather more casually on his thin long frame, like he doesn't put much effort into it. but his presence feels good.

he's got a bit of me in him.

i usually control my reactions upon his arrival. we won't wave at each other. he just comes and sits beside me, nudging me a bit with his shoulder as a way of saying hello between us, not realising that it actually became a thing over time. that nudge loosens me up and i release my nails from my mouth that i wasn't aware of biting in the first place.

i know his name but never really tested it on my tongue, saying it out loud. but just his presence and his body beside me every Sunday evening when i'm tired of normalcy of life seems more than enough. There are no accusations or expectations. Just the derision - the uncertain gratification of his presence. and i guess mine too, for him?

its freezing but he's always wearing this thin black leather jacket that doesn't really help much i think. but i feel he chooses to feel cold. he likes it - but i've never really known someone enjoy winter and snow so literally.

his black worn out leather jacket and mud rusted gum boots remind me a bit too much of warm milk and honey and cookies or a warm cup of coffee on a lazy weekend in your bed - waking up with the things that make you feel safe around you, waking up to no alarm but just a soft reminder that your mind and body is well rested, really waking up to nothing ahead of you, nowhere to rush, nowhere to go. just nothing.

time kind of decided to terminate.

and its suppose to be painful, but the slow pace of time has never been this addicting. its like you're in this phase of sleeping where you're not awake and you're not sleeping, but you're having this dream that almost feels real.

he takes out this cheap bottle of vodka, the one that comes in transparent glass bottles and shares back and forth with me. i try and sketch, for the only time, without thinking of actually creating something, or coming out with something - but i just sketch. he flogs himself with nicotine and gulps down vodka - looking around.

there are a few too silent looks and eye locks and shrugs exchanged, almost questioning each other's presence every Sunday evening, with no answers, but neither failing to notice the smudged smile on the other's face every time such expressions are exchanged.

a smile that's a secret and is not meant to be seen by the other.

and somewhere around in those not so promising and uncertain looks exchanged - that heavy and uncomfortable feeling in my chest takes its silent departure. it leaves me to myself. i feel blank and empty every Sunday evening. a blank and empty i crave through the next 6 days. a blank and empty that is somehow always there in this moment in his presence.

an hour passes, which feels like a whole day, and he gets up to leave, he looks at me one time and mumbles a faint thanks thats probably just meant for his own satisfaction and for his own ears. But it flatters a kind of fondness and warmth all over my chest and i give a friendly shrug. i sit for another 10 minutes, dreading to face the next 6 days and already waiting for next Sunday.

i really am not in love with him. he's not a friend. he's not a dorm mate or a family member - and i cannot label him, because his worth seems to be way beyond that.

i get high on this random strangers' presence every Sunday evening, abiding a goodbye without promising to be there next week, which surprisingly doesn't increase that uncertainty in my heart and head like it should. its surprisingly certain, and promising.

his presence is a promise.

To Die, with Love

people usually stick around to watch you grow, to watch you climb up and succeed - to watch you live, and laugh.

do you love me enough to stick around and watch me die, tho?

i had to make her die - *with love.*

i read to her sometimes, i got her sketchpad and charcoal for her, she didn't have much energy but her hands were the same. a little dead on the outside, but the printed creativity on the paper whispered life, and love, and happy things like existence, and stolen kisses.

she read the sweetest poetry i've ever heard, her lips sliding like brush against paint.

i didn't have to look at the clock to know how many days were left. her body spoke to me enough. every day her lips turned paler and her body thinner, but her eyes, - her eyes stayed the same, the same sharp blue stared at me every single morning from the bed in the hospital.

that look was worth getting up for.

i watched her eat, and draw, and sleep. there were dark brown patches under her eyes, and freckles on her nose, and i smiled every time i looked at them - *she's so damn beautiful.*

and once in a while i cried, you know there are moments that change the way your very soul exists? That changes your very definition of happiness and all your favourite songs?

i was holding her hand, and we sat beside each other on cold hospital chairs. the typical smell of bland food flooded our senses. i was staring out the window, the sun and the birds nulled the pain a little. i was numb. i looked at her and she was playing with my left hand, my fingers and my palm, and small spots on my wrist, and i had this sudden urge of just killing myself, or maybe dying with her on her waiting death bed.

she put her head down, facing away from me, with my hand underneath her cheek, pale and warm, and it just - fit - the curve of her cheek and the sharp point of her cheekbone against the warmth of my palm.

i put my head down too, facing her. and i didn't mean to, but i started crying, tiny sobs, praying that she doesn't hear me, because God, i had to be strong for her.

my face felt wet and my clothes were too hot and both my palms were sweaty. she turned her head in my direction and now her other cheek rested on my sweaty palm. i flinched for a moment.

i didn't want her to see me cry - she deserved better than that.

but not for a second did she frown, or look angry, or sad and -

- and she passed me this smile i reckon I'd dream of every single time I'd look at happy colours and sad smiles.

she smiled at me like she was grateful. she literally looked past my tears, she ignored them and in a way wiped them without even touching them, she made their presence null, like they don't exist. the sun reflected her skin and it fucking shone an impossibly beautiful shade of 'existence' - if that was a colour.

"you've got sad eyes with a hint of braveness," is all she said, "- i got you." her voice a bare whisper but the firmest sentence she had formed.

that moment changed my life.

small tears welled in my eyes, rolling down my cheeks in an endless flare, capturing on my top lip and slipping through the smallest crevice between my pursed lips,

our bodies have grown together,

it was a pleasure to know her, to fall in love with her, to spend the best moments of my life with her, and to watch her die,

how many people can you name that make you feel like that?

i didn't even try to stop my tears. i cried for hours on end, and she just rested her cheek on my palm, played with my fingers, and smiled at me.

"*my mouth's a mixture of 100 different disgusting medicines.*" she told me every single time.

i kissed her hard any way.

its always like a first with you.

she'd flinch when i touched her bare waist, inner thighs, or arms. and then i touched her again, firmer. and then she'd give up. she'd shrink and hide herself in my arms. she'd whisper inaudible things in my neck - like her memory from her 10th birthday, and sometimes she'd cry. her tears were beautiful. and sometimes she was angry, and she'd blurt an inaudible chorus of impressive curses.

my body has grown with you.

she smelled of the beautiful ink carved on her skin, she smelled of her art, of the uncountable paintings hung and starched in every corner of our home, she smelled of pain and deprivation, and she smelled of love.

she's permanently grown on me.

she's everything wonderful. she's like a calming moon during the daytime and the lustrous shiny sun at midnight. she's just something else. she's my language, she's my consistent prayer. she's my safe word, and she's the whole of me.

i love her enough to watch her die - you're the perfect end to the life I'm yet to live.

Stale Pages

it was raining and i was away from my family. thousands miles apart. it was so cold. the kind you felt on the inside of your skin, the kind you can't warm with clothes or heat. the kind that stays and just, stays. its like a layer inside you, travelling, journaling its way through your mind, your bones, your toes, your ears, you. i just needed to be kissed. i went out barefoot, my ears hurt because of the cold wind, my feet numb and my fingers clutched in fists. i wouldn't cry. i was beyond that point.

i looked up and the sky was beautiful. i saw the water droplets on leaves - pink, yellow, orange, blue. i picked up one red leaf and kept it in my hand just because i needed to hold something, and that leaf looked warm. my vision blurred, my glasses were fogged and my hair was wet. the cold i felt on the outside of my skin was somehow so warm. i'm not sure if its odd to pray to catch a cold or fever, but i did. but thats me. i'm odd. my eyelids ached and that felt good too. i kept walking until i craved my blanket again, or a cup of coffee. anything to kill this hollowness.

i still think i just needed to be kissed, or hugged, or talked to. about ordinary dreams, failures, about bridges and red rare bushes. about souls and personalities - broken personalities - and how they are fixable. how sadness isn't here to stay but it might take a while. how some days you need to be on your own and just make it to the end of the day or cry it all out on your own because friends aren't always there beside you. i just feel so deeply for everything, and i'm not sure if there's anything scarier than that. because this is life. its cold and harsh with cracks of warmth and softness.

i'm tired. really tired. *wrap your blanket around yourself and think of a good memory, about a palm on the circle of your head or the curve of your cheek, or a hand around your waist. think of the last line of your favourite song and pray for numbness. and slip.* i'm tired. really tired. i should sleep.

i slept. i dreamed of words. *can you mend me?*

Over a Cup of Coffee

the rough brisk of dirty snow and small rumbles of rain drops on the window shell weren't loud enough to numb the warmth in my chest and the faint sound of *its calling, i just want one more day with you* from the open door of the bathroom.

i knew this was it.

i looked around the room - his room - which was lightened by the dullness of the moon through the window and the golden shade of side bed lamps.

i saw my miserable textbooks stocked at the end of the bed with dirty sheets smelling too much like musky sex. i saw my glasses on the side table that had made a little home right there since the day i met him, and two used coffee mugs on the window aisle with coffee stains on the white wall, and a collection of my used clothes dumped in the corner of the room.

coffee, i thought, and smiled.

it was his room - but it felt more like 'ours' now.

it was christmas time and we were both packing to go back home for christmas but it felt too much like leaving home instead - and that made me realise that this is such a wrong moment.

but that's me.

i'm not right. i'm the wrong in everything. i'm not big roses and expensive wine and impressive clothes and a mouth lusty cologne accompanied by a big banner of 'will you marry me?' — i'm the wrong, i'm different pairs of socks and trousers hanging low on my hips that belong to him and early morning sugary creamy coffee and silent hitches and worn out oxford books, i'm fucking silent, i'm simple. i'm not eye contacts and confidence, i'm fear and doubts and I'm hesitancy but a firm hesitancy, i'm just - just simple.

"babe," it was a rumpled whisper but was more than enough to get his shy attention and have him padding out the bathroom door with a towel hanging low around his hips.

he had toothpaste foam smudged on his upper lip with his hair going into a million different directions but his eyes - *his fucking eyes* - a yummy brown like honey drizzled over chocolate and a *lets watch the sun come up* - that made me feel like this is it.

he climbed on the bed and didn't think twice before joining our lips in a random kiss - a random kiss for survival. the tongue play gave me a chance to squeak out my hand under the pillow and get out the worn out black box.

i shoved the ring box messily into his hands and the abrupt break of our kiss made me even more nervous. his face an expression i couldn't name even if i tried, it was a *what* and *how* and an uncertain *i'm in love with you.*

"just open it."

he opened the box and it was the slowest ten seconds of my life, it was *lets crawl in naked and forget there's a world outside and beyond us* and *mess of tangled legs and nudges of toes against the arch of the foot.*

the cheap christmas lights reflectively danced on his face and his skin almost cerulean against the moon's light. he was the most beautiful existence of life i'd ever seen.

he looked at me with an abashed grin and a shameless shock of kiss which was more *tongue and teeth and laugh and smile* rather than just lips. it was my favourite kind.

we parted and he - he just fucking looked at me like i'm the shining moon he needs to look at before sleeping or the morning coffee he can't go a day without.

coffee, i thought, and smiled.

and amidst all this mess of a human emotion named love, with my eyes on my hands in my lap, i spoke,

"it took me a year to just look into your eyes and ask you how your day was and a year and a half to get your coffee right and two years to kiss you and fuck you out of your senses without any hesitancy, and i just.."

i remember staying silent for exact 4.5 seconds, and i thought is it possible that the person who loves you is capable of filling in the silence with shaded fluffs of fond and love and maybe something like *support*.

"and i can't believe i didn't go down on my knees, or wore a pretty dress, or wait for until at least you finished your bath to fucking propose you or even now i can't look into your eyes and, b…but, i… i'm…"

i tried to remember breathing was a thing, and it felt like i hadn't seen his face for hours now.

i was just so scared.

but he was so damn worth it, he deserved eye contacts and a firm assurance of love and something like a beginning of another family in the crowded roar of London, so i looked up,

"but i'm in love with you, man, i'm so arse over tits in love with you. my morning coffee doesn't taste the same if you're not sitting with me by the window and i fucking can't imagine waking up and not getting a kiss from you with your mouth full of that foamy toothpaste and just… let me stick around for a lifetime, alright? like, your life means more to me than it does to you and its unfair but just… just marry me, yeah?"

i always took pride in knowing what i say and being aware but i just realised the basics of proposing and it means you ask a person to marry you and i suppose i maybe just told him to marry me, but,

oh, well..

thats all my eyes could take.

his breathy and wet laugh was a sight not to miss but i still didn't look up. i was holding back my own fond and sobs, and it was hard.

"hold that thought," - was all i got and before i could look up he had wandered off into the kitchen with the towel almost falling off from hips and although his walk was jumpy and full of life, i felt a dull ache in my chest and a *what if i fucked up*.

the next 7.8 minutes were a word, *numb*. and somehow my eyes were permanently fixated on my laps and hands.

a yummy steam and a warm cup was placed ungracefully on my hands and i looked up to see him sitting in front of me with his cup of coffee, his hands in his laps and the box of ring clutched tightly in his palm and a grin radiating an annoying level of happiness.

"this moment was kinda incomplete without coffee, yeah?" he whispered and it was the most beautiful bunch of vowels to ever come out of his mouth.

he looked at me and just - *it felt like a yes.*

loud certainty and commitment, it was such a fucking 'yes'.

his knuckles brushed softly against my cheek and none cared to point or wipe or kiss the wetness in each other's eyes.

"i know its too simple and not grand or dramatic but…"

"- but its so *us*." he completed for me, with tainted pink cheeks and a red nose and dried toothpaste foam on his upper lip and *God*, i was going to embarrass myself by having a breakdown. he *was so goddamn beautiful.*

he kissed my thumb and the dents of my fingers and placed the cool shiny metal on my palm like a 'yes', again.

i took his hand and slid the ring and i should feel nervous and scared and think about all the things that could go wrong but what i felt was a pulsing heart in my throat and understanding the clichéd meaning of two bodies and a single soul.

normal proposals had grand kisses and amazing sex at the end of it all but it was just coffee.

coffee, i thought, and smiled.

coffee and us, and thats quite enough.

So, What Did Your Kiss Taste Like?

there are very few things in this world that change you as a person, as a soul - like dreams, loss of your loved ones, affection, achievements, and - and *kisses*. you're never the same once you've been kissed. not just kissed. *but really kissed.* its just not a slimy spit exchange, its more tongue intercourse, its more *building* something together - like a future, a bond - a moment to be cherished forever.

we shall take this journey together - the bumps and the slides - the walks and the rides - just you and me - and our kisses,

its a piece of art - is what it is.

Its an actual blessed imprint of someone else's very own soul, their sayings and bits of their life into your system

he tastes like cigarettes, and the chocolates he always nicks from the cupboard of his dorm, the stale banana he ate and the bitter black coffee he must've had on his way to the class,

i can dig a faint taste of mint toothpaste too, and scented dried sweat on the corner of his lips

— the delicious aroma leaving me salivating

its all bits of him in me.

these were just things before, normal things - the mint toothpaste, coffee, cigarettes, chocolates, but now i realise that these are some of my favourite things.

i could also taste the unsaid apologies and the forced lies, the hidden affection and ashamed confessions

the kiss all naked - lips sliding, sulking, swooning against mine

drunk sound of skin against skin, and kill me, kill me if that isn't the most beautiful sound in the whole wide world

his mouth was a new home i was given the chance to explore, a home i'm gonna sneak in every AM and PM

flag a permanent pair of footsteps - mine, all mine.

mess of limbs - fingers and nails, two pair of sandy feet

a petite waist held by a firm grip

adams apple bobbing - his growls and coos,

her whines and moans,

a closeness in which you can't decipher where one begins and the other ends.

its oneness. its one whole soul coming together with every slick of tongue, and every harsh breath snatched from each lung

may i ask you now,

have you ever *really* been kissed?

if yes, then i please to know - what is it like?

is it a last? *full of side tracked tears, water afresh, and salt that surprisingly doesn't sting* or is it a first? *random well fitted plump softness against yours, and a slick familiar taste of saliva that feels too much like home*

is it in an between need? *an addictive pressure needed against yours at random hours,*

is it a reminder? *drowning in an exaggerated content sigh of relief, and contentment*

or is it a promise? *a welcomed painful press before parting ways*

is it a lie? *a rhythm shouting a well rehearsed put on show*

or is it a silent deed of appreciation? *a tranquil gesture of plain happiness made upon realisation of your blessings*

or is it just - new? *a novel language that doesn't exist and is too special to be known by everyone, a language that settles in your mouth to make a home, a language that's unsettling at first but too fluent to let go, a language that's here to stay,*

or it could be a speechless moment? *communicating something words cannot, sharing something that doesn't have a name or a term in human dictionary*

or is it just a random thing? *that roasted smell of faded detergent that's just so him - or maybe his favourite pasta flavour lingering in dents of his teeth - a thing that's just him*

i don't want to know your name, or where you come from. don't tell me your hobbies. don't tell me your favourite colour or your philosophical 3 am thoughts. don't tell me about your heartbreak or bitch of a best friend that you have. don't tell me about your favourite book or that you're a homophobe. just tell me about your goddamn kiss.

the kiss that changed you.

the kiss that put the high offered by all drugs and alcohol to shame, that made your walls stronger but also made you realise that you're not sitting alone in the four walled room, there's someone right beside you, that made you smile with crumbs of fries falling off your mouth and making you crinkle your eyes without being insecure about the wrinkles it forms on your cheeks,

how the slide of lips hugged your fears and made them your friends, how the bite of his teeth shared your happiness and doubled it over, how the sucking of his tongue divided your sadness and filled your empty cup full of vibrant colours and a dare - a dare to make you live,

the kiss that made you be you.

so - what did your kiss taste like?

sketch1.jpg

Shave down There

he always looked at me like he loved me

    but he always asked me to shave myself

    down there

    i arched an eye brow and looked at it

    waiting for him to

    just

    just fucking leave the room for a bit

    i'm not sure if i said that out loud

    i lied down, taking off my pants and shoving up my cardigan

    sliding my hand past my navel into the curls

    playing and twisting

    "is it not okay to look like this?"

    i whispered to myself, myself - down there

    i waited for an answer that never came and the ghosts of his words surrounded me strong. a snicker of light drew my attention and i looked at the ceiling to floor mirror on my right.

i saw myself.

every time my hand moved into the curls between my inner thighs, around, up, down, or inside, there was a sneer of reflection from the sun that bounced back from the mirror.

fuck

it looked beautiful.

i looked beautiful.

the black contrasted magically with the bounces of light and i felt dizzy on my own self. the slick of sweat in between the spaces of my fingers smoothened the grip and the pull and i thought about safeness and being your own rope of strength. i thought about originality and loving yourself raw, without layers of fabric or colour, or even skin. i couldn't take my eyes off myself.

and i wondered, sadly

how many women fail to love themselves like this?

i went to sleep thinking of how beautiful i really am - down there, and that i wouldn't change a thing about it if i wanted to.

and if he walks in on me naked with my hand stuck in the curls in my clit, and wishes to walk out, i reckon i'd wake up a twisted degree happier.

River of a Girl

the pages of the book flew abandoned and he just stared at them fly and flap and make all kinds of noises.

they did something. something wrong. something evil.

they told him a story that moved him. he can't believe his eyes. he has never cried in his life. because, boys don't cry, do they?

they told him a story of a girl that lived in this small town with purple trees and an unnamed river that did wonders for a soul. she went near the old river that no one bothered with because it was old. and old things bore people. aged things don't charm people. and that's exactly why she went to the river. because it was old and aged, it had rocks from hundreds of years ago and it's water flowed as if with every round its wanting to tell the stories of all kinds of people that visited the river and deposited trash into it from ashes of deeds to cigarettes.

but the girl,

she was a little different,

every day she visited the river and painted the sight. everything same, from the placement of the trees to the nuance of the sky, the only thing that changed was the shade of the water, in every single painting, the waves a different design every day, and every different gradation, the same glisten of the water with a different luminosity every single day ; like she was the only one that really got the river... really got the stories it tried to tell people all these years.

stories about a man drowned deep a thousand feet, or a woman raped behind the bush. stories about lovers making love or holding hands near the rock, a girl crying because she broke her mothers' heart to a boy with a broken soul.

but he doesn't know what made him cry, maybe it was her appreciation for nature, or her devotion towards her art, or just the way she existed. her stillness moved mountains in his chest and drops of water slid gracefully down his cheeks.

buys don't fucking cry

but i wish i followed my art every day

i wish i kept my promises more often

i wish i talked to my mom a little more

i wish i appreciated the butterflies a little bit more

over and above that i just wish i appreciated life more

he looked at the pages of the book, still flapping. the worn out edges and the same pungent woody scent of the flattened book. he'd been sitting at the same spot, still having moved miles within - and ten steps closer to his real self.

he murmurs to his mom,

"i cried, mom,"

and a voice came,

"i'm proud of you,"

Unusual

you. my unusual beauty. my quiet, quiet man,

you,

wondering aimlessly

the taste of pink flavoured drinks

and roads of oxford street,

obsessing with Lang Leav or her memories

wearing jumpers that haven't been washed because we love the smell of 'used'

you made me realise that quiet is the best kind of wild and that not all loud things have to be screaming and shouting, a quiet i've known to kiss over the years, and for what i'll always be thankful. but you, my unusual beauty, my quiet, quiet man

smoking cigars

the puffs looking a mayhem of pink and purple with a shading of black and white

and my quiet, quiet man,

you're a painting made of colours not worth being touched

breathing like electricity and gaze like fire

your silence quiet like calm unbounded pages of a book

wearing caps with a knob head or scarves with holes

or loving libraries with a crowd and restaurants just before the closing hours

wrapped up in thick blankets at 34 degrees and nakedness in a -2

you made me realise that kindness is after all a selfish act of self instead of selflessness.

a truth i've grown to realise more with time and every day passing, a truth people don't tell each other for they live to get off their good images and acts of kindness, a truth i'll always be thankful to you for.

you find unusual love only once in a lifetime, the kind of love that makes you realise all the above. realise the bitterness of kindness or the secrets attached behind labels. the unusual love that doesn't ask for permission before clearing your dark spots and leaving.

just leaving mid way for they never made promises, for they don't believe in words like forever and always, and you realise you've been fixed. fixed like rock bottom hard and you're not broken anymore. and your unusual fond isn't all that around to thank or love

for your quiet man needn't believe in words like forever and always and instead believe in a love of quality and a love of good

not a love of time and a love thats to be 'managed'

my quiet, quiet man taught me the unusual silence which no one has. everyone is just ready to fight with as many weapons, knives and brains and egos. but who lives with silence? my quiet, quiet man, smoking cigars with pink smoke, defying beauty of orchids, and falling for the soft fingers of his that stroke - beautiful, beautiful pages of my existence.

Life's Good

i remember sitting at the table and thinking about not moving. not even a single thing. the turkey on the sides with mashed potatoes and flower pot in the centre.

my dad's laugh radiated off the glasses of the windows, whilst he filled himself another glass of champagne. his hands grow with mine and somehow my hands feel the same size as they were when i was a little kid and held his hand. i feel like my hand or his hand hasn't grown since, or maybe grown together.

my mother cuts the turkey and i think salmon, rose pink and prime pale red. she keeps her palm on the top of my knuckles, right where my anxiety marks are and that's just my bandage. her boundless motherhood, from baby cribs to my single bed at the university and remembering her rare prodigious hands as i burn food in the kitchen every day. she puts a piece of turkey on my plate but I'm not hungry. so i look into her eyes and right there's my health within them, there's my well being and so much care and now i'm hungry.

i look at my elder brother and think of all the years we didn't talk because we grew apart like sometimes two people just do and i think there's nothing sadder than that for his blood runs in my veins. but then i look at him again and i'm thankful, i'm thankful because he sits right beside and i can smell care beaming off his being and we have a few years, or so i pray to bring back the time evaporated and inventing an unforgettable recollection of memories. of a childhood we should've had together.

i failed this year in my high school and i'm repeating it. i got my result today. i've started therapy and this is my third week. it doesn't help me. i'm hugging hope day night and i'm praying some day hope might decide to hug me right back.

but as i sit here and i look at them, i think of chances and things happening for good. and sometimes failures being the actual win. i think of love and what really matters at the end of the day. the set up around me in the name of a home, a friend who'd come on my single timid cry and

and a family.

these are my words but these are my different faces too so look at me when i say this - if you have a family, you, my love, have everything in this world. everything.

i look at them and i think

i think life's good.

really good.

I Remember

i remember always being so warm around him

    with his hands as a coat and his lips as a shield over mine

    the warm of his lips tell me he's been hurt quite a lot, i want to hold his hand but somewhere it doesn't feel enough, somewhere i think some kinds of pain are meant to stay, they are meant to be a part of somebody's soul, they are meant to ache you once in a while

    the rain wet my lips and when i kiss the warmth of his i feel we don't fit

    we're that imperfection in perfection and the annoying wetness in a dry world

    we're that piece of glass in your skin you can never find

    we're defeated, uneven, shattered - in the best way

    sometimes you meet a person that's not meant to heal you, you meet the person because you share the same ache in each others' bones, and — and when you kiss, only for a second, the ache subsides and there's a sigh of relief on both the sides and that — that's the whole point.

In the Castle

its the castle we made with snow and wet mud sometimes,

over warm tea dates and pasta licks, some lazy kisses in the end and a shared umbrella,

its my alternate universe where there's a castle of wet sand and snow, a castle with big gates, yards of green around

you're that little boy i met when the snow storm came and i escaped my bed

you're that little boy who made me fall in love with snow. who told me snow's capable of making heart shapes and stars that i search for in the sky every once in a while. you told me snow's capable of radiating warmth between two souls. i furrowed my eyebrows when you said that, and you simply smiled. you took off our gloves and the cold pierces my fingertips, you latched our hands to one another and it almost felt like i was feeding off your skin. the lava burn between our palms caused a dull ball of excitement between my legs and *oh.*

oh,

the thing that burns between us will always be our little flame of a secret and i'm in love with snow now, i'm in love with the warmth that comes with it. the white shine of it so glossy and crystal, like small wishes you make upon broken eyelids

you're that abandoned broken eyelid i'll always, always make a wish upon

you're kisses i'll never forget and hugs i'll always need to heal

you're that one wish i'll chase all day every day in the church, that one i won't ever give up on.

Connection

sometimes you're just connected to a person. sometimes you're just attached to the hip metaphorically and that's all there is, there's moaning and shameless sex, there's confessions of her exhibitionist kink and secrets of his lost limb in the war. there's smiles through old phone calls and a small "i think he'd like that" before everything that you do. sometimes, you part in the morning for work with a kiss thats a temporary goodbye but also a tiny bit permanent cause *what if*. sometimes, you're complete but never really calmly whole. you're never really okay, with a big part of your existence walking around free in the cruel world.

A rose for You, Ma'am

i was on my way to my home - no - my house.

the rose brushes the inside of my wrist as the kid hands me the rose walks away silently.

i hope some day someone hands you a rose and tells you, "its for free, keep it."

i hope that someone doesn't ask for money, or a favour. just simply hands you the rose and leaves. you look at the rose and think how much you needed this.

i touch my wrist, where the scars lay hidden, i think of my planned future, some new scars and some pain relief.

then, then i look at the rose. its not the best kind. the petals are fading into an old, rotten red, and the stem is bent and the leaves are home for a couple of ants. and suddenly i'm transferred into this alternate universe where this rose is me. i'm the petal. the scars on my wrist are ants that feed off the leaves and i'm suddenly reminded by the boy that

you're soft, did you know?

you're the soft of the petal. the velvety touches and kisses lingered on the petals by the world. the feel of it under the fingertips, all mushy and tender. you're that gentle petal. you're that kind piece of rose that keeps the broken heart going, you're a token of love exchanged all over the universe.

but then i think of stems, of ant eaten leaves, of the broken tail of the flower - which forces me to think of the beauty of the petal. none of it lessens the beauty of the petal. and it never will.

you, my darling, are a rose.

and i feel, maybe, maybe i want to reduce my scars - maybe i want to relish my petals, my velvet skin that i abuse.

maybe,

maybe i want to fall in love with myself.

Our Existence

my body breathes in your existence.
>there's heat coiling deep in my stomach
>a warmth between my thighs
>a soft tremble to my spine
>a bite to my lip
>*my body lives in your existence*

Little Darkness

the sun shines but it still doesn't for some.

they're amongst us, head low and walking in their own darkness. fighting the lonesome game of not belonging.

and i want to fall in love with a someone like you

Don't Love

sometimes love is in the things you don't do.

the kiss you don't give. the hand you let go, the arm you hold back, the cry you don't sob, the pain you don't allow to ache, the heart you don't allow to live

sometimes love

is letting go

sketch2.jpg

What About Them?

what about the ones that are left behind? the millions that don't make it? the souls shattered and dreams broken.

no, really

what about them?

where's my home?

Be Okay

somedays i want to be okay with you being sad, little, and scared.

    i know it was on a weekend you lost control, your little secrets about scratching your skin. the scars on your arm and inner thighs seem like letters to me. letters made of alphabets people refuse to read or notice. maybe they are scared. they are scared for the scars are so strong. you are so strong. so maybe i am okay with you being sad. however, it doesn't stop my little efforts to make you smile, with the tea a little too hot and my protective arm around your petite little shoulder, with extra honey in your coffee inhaling your exhaled air every night. and i think i'm okay because i feel sometimes its meant to be this way, some souls are meant to be partially sad.

My Hopeful Week

on Monday i hop onto the last fleet of stairs and look at strangers on their way to a destination. on Tuesday i wave at a stranger i find looking a little sad. he doesn't wave back. on Wednesday i wave at a stranger that looks a little happy. she doesn't wave back either. on Thursday and Friday i wave at a bunch of office workers that look are having their lunch. they notice me but don't wave back. on Saturday, i get a little sad, i don't wave at anyone, hoping for someone to wave at me. at night, i cry myself to sleep.

on Sunday, i hope, i hope to hope, and on Monday, *i wave again.*

Beauty and Blood

i lost control on a weekend. i burnt flames into my skin on a dark Saturday night, at 12 am there were ashes of cigarettes melting my skin.

i found it beautiful.

A Shining Friend

you're the unknown friends that the stars have

    the unknown friend no one knows about

    the stars turn to you when they are bleeding a little

    and loving these stars is like sitting on a cushion of stones but you don't complain

I Don't Know Anymore

your hands are the bandage to my wound
    but you're the colour of my blood
    and i don't know how this works

I Don't Belong

it left a few scars

    the words they said

    somewhere along the lines of i don't belong

    the chair is not for you

    the table doesn't have your name

    you're not allowed to hold the flower

    your skin could be fairer

    eyes darker

    nails shorter and clothes brighter

    your smile could be like hers and hair like him

    you could be like someone else

    you could be anything but you

    but why?

    the whisper so soft

    why? am i not alright?

    you are

    but i wish you'd remind yourself that a little more often

Somewhere Midway

i'm scared. i always need something to do

i fear if i have nothing to do, i'll end up floating in vacant air with heavy gulps of lump and a lot of confusion. no news about a right or a left or a yes or a no. no news about the time of the day,

i've got the blanket bundled around my thigh. i tossed and turned the entire night. my favourite lights were on but when i looked at them, suddenly light was about darkness and dullness. the cooked salmon i tried to eat had a small creature coming from underneath. the pen i wrote with stopped working and my assignment file got deleted on its own

i have nothing to do now, except to wait and see the light again. i breath but its heavy and i count every breath like a stone on water. its like writing but not being able to understand the meaning of your own words and its like a book with an exciting cover but blank pages within. i can't stop trembling.

emptiness shouldn't have to be this scary.

Math

plus doesn't wish to add and minus refuses to subtract

divider hates being a half and multiplication hates the number two itself

i allow you to be

i allow you to fall in love

to make a friend

to do what you love

i free you from what you're assigned

Alternate Universe

i allow all the country colours to come together today

    the sunflower to shy the way it wants and the rose to move with grace

    and the grace of the rose reminds me of you, the way the sunflower changes its sight, the way its yellow is tinted to a bright pink,

    the shy of sunflower and grace of rose

    its like they breed

    they breed to love

    they breed to create and accept

    altruism nature of the grass beneath

    whistle of the wind

    kisses of the mountains

    the clouds puff out some smoke

    some mist and a few drops of rain

    the sun beams a unicorn white and the mood a shiny yellow

    the rose and the sunflower sway together

the shyness does a pirouette of fond and the grace, a twirl of affection

there's so much love

this is an alternate universe

The Death I Fear

i fear one day i might die a death
    a death where i stop *creating art*

Hiding

i saw

    i saw how you hid behind your lashes

    behind kind things like a smile or a wet laughter

    some snort down your upper lip and wet eyelids sticking together

    moist eyes and

    and you look a little tired.

    he looks at you like he's studying you and you adjust your bangs right in front of your eyes

    and then i think maybe you're not hiding

    maybe

    maybe you were really just blinding yourself

    blinding yourself from the world

    i'm glad you're staying safe

Stop Looking

you've been limping in love a while too long
    and i'm praying for you
        the day he'll stop looking for gold in you
        is the day he'll actually find it

Let Your Feathers Grow

your thighs remind me of white chocolate

a hint of amber in between your clit and there's honey dripping down your knee

soft is all i think

feathers are all i feel

there's a tree within you

your roots are capable of so much

you hide it like you're ashamed of it

but really

let your feathers head for the hills

sway for the lakes and flee for the sky

let yourself fly

The Box

the box was all the things and you. some old photographs and an ancient pocket watch with a cracked glass. the cracks looked like a sketch of your face and i wanted to cry. there were the bands you used to tie your hair back because smallest of things can mess you your focus and that abandoned camera you picked up whilst we were on a walk together from the middle of the road because such precious things don't deserve to be abandoned.

Staring, a While

staring, you've been staring at the computer screen a while
  your eyes are red rimmed
  and it seems you've been writing vigorously
  not sure
  whether
  to save yourself
  or
  this world

Never Fallen This Hard

i remember eating leftovers with you, leftovers of students in the back of the canteen.

you're our age but you don't study with us. you study in the kitchen day and night and needless to say there's magic in your hands. i lick your fingers clean and later we lie under the shiny steel table and pretend the head of the table is the sky and the shine, the stars. we pretend the stink of unwashed utensils is actually the aroma of rawness and excitement, like a mixture of the smell of gift wrapping paper and purple scented butterfly.

nothing has changed about the town we live in. there's this feeling of déjà vu in my nerves when we walk through the field of crops and suddenly its raining. we don't try to hide because we never get beautiful skies to us. we've had table of steels for rooftops and now i want to kiss the sky through your soul. with you its like the future has already happened and the past is yet to exist. with you there's home and things like my favourite mug and my favourite type of leftover we eat once everyone's eaten.

and i know

i've never fallen this hard before

Your Lower Lip

i love holding your lower lip between my fingertips

    as we drive through the lanes of the windy country side

    it goes lax and soft

    mumbling muted words

    that you never said

    yawning your way through the nights

    smiling into the sunshine

    the dented windows help me to steal a kiss or a moment of love

    my forefinger touches the tip of your tongue

    its damp like kept too long in the pouring rain

    the drops drizzle across my face

    as we drive through the lanes of the windy country sides

    your lower lip trembles sometimes

    it shakes with dread of losing our breed of love and hollow things like death

    i cease the tremble of your lower lip

and mutter

"we're away from life driving on a country side lane

the breeze flees like it supports us and our car hasn't stopped once like its gonna be there

the fruits we stole from the field melt like honey on our tongues and darling nothing,

nothing could go wrong."

the dull cushions under your eyes take a turn back and the lines on your forehead soothe like you were waiting for my voice

nothing could go wrong.

Not Right

he's not right for you
    your lucky stars said

    i know

    you murmured

    kissing my blood

The Way You Sleep

your spit runs down my shirt and your head lolls an inch higher on my shoulder

    eyelids heavy and lashes all dark

    the man on the aisle looks at you like you're weird

    i look at him like maybe he shouldn't exist

    i think i see birds in the window behind your head

    they look at you sleep on my shoulder

    and offer their feathers like quills which we could write our love story with

    the colour of their skin like ink and coating of their body like paper

    their eyes tell me it shows

    it shows how much i love you

    at night

    the celestial constellations scare me

    because they look at me like they know my secret

    of this untold world i've created

where,

you and i - don't exist

we - do

where

us - is all there is

Its Worth It

its worth it
- if my words shine for you - even if they don't for me
- its worth it
- if the moon hides on some days
- with stars full of selfish wishes from around the universe
- its worth it
- if i bleed
- and that makes your heart beat
- its worth it
- if my breathing slacks
- and the colour of your eyes brightens
- if i die typing you a letter i would never send
- its worth it

The Little Moon

the little moon doesn't hold any more secrets

    its not a liar like us

    it knows the rights and the wrongs but it goes beyond it

    some are born for the rights

    some for the wrongs

    some for neither

    some, to go beyond right and wrong

    some - to go for unreachable galaxies and horizons of the globe

    some - to change the world for themselves

    and some - to change the world, for the world

    i need to go home

    as i sip tea on an aircraft to a country i know nothing about

    i think of my mom

    her warmth and her warnings of do's and don'ts

my surroundings suddenly hit too close to home and i don't know what to do

i bite into the edge of the cup because i feel a lot and i had a vodka with coke a while back

i lost my spectacles under the table, looking right and left, people refused to help me

and i think of a sudden warm hand always there for help, a ghost of breath you remember too well, a familiar rush of blood that runs in your veins, and hands that are always, always there to help, like a soft hand on the shoulder when you're crouched down sobbing your life away in tears and two hands under your armpits because you lost control

and as i sip tea on an aircraft to a country i know nothing about

i think of warm hands

hands that never grow old for me and always stay the same way

the warmth and the warning of do's and don't's

the bite

the bite on the edge of the cup is a proof

a proof

that

that i've missed a little too much

and i need to go home

My Ink

ink on my skin is how i remember

    the cups, the hearts

    a little phoenix and the pattern that reminds me of my culture

    there's something about black over my skin

    the white shading on the borders and the dissolving of memories into the layers of my being

    there's something

    something about my skin beneath the ink

    its not like the rest on my body

    its rather milky, in contrast to the darkness, its soft to touch and sometimes

    sometimes i'd lick it in desperation

    to remind myself of that moment

    because ink on my skin is how i remember

the cups, the hearts

a little phoenix

a little

little doodle

inked on my skin, a little doodle, *called home*

Sometimes

sometimes i think if god didn't create a you and a i but instead just an 'us'

    and when we

    we come together

    with my back to your front

    all bare

    it would feel like the prickles on my skin grow and lick the surface of your being

    like two skins joining together

    like two souls being born again

    like no you and i

    like just, and just an 'us'

    and that if your arms and legs are paralysed

    i could be your sensation

    placing my hand on the back of your neck i'd murmur

"take me around the world on your wheelchair, let me sit in your lap and be your paralysis, let me keep my head on your shoulder and touch the points on your body where we always feel our skins connecting... let me..."

As Kids

the snowman we created as kids dissolved into the ice but never melted from my memories. there was a box we kept, of photographs we stole from our parents, because we wanted some memories to ourselves rather than putting them framed on display for the world.

we've always stored memories, haven't we? like the buttons of the snowman that never melted for me and maybe you or the time i cut myself into unconsciousness and the first thing after opening my eyes was see you, crouched down and face happy because i was gonna be okay. because you found me before it got too late. we stored that blade, you said it was a symbol of strength for the both of us. funny how we never found trophies appealing but rather the warm hugs we gave each other at the end of the races we lost and competitions that told us we're not good enough. the christmas parties at school with the old music player was what everyone loved but i remember away from the human breed in the last classroom on the fifth floor, banging the tables and slapping the foot, clapping our hands with echoes of laughter radiating off halls and no intention of silencing. we kept the pieces of chalks we threw at each other too and the way we told ourselves that our noses kissing is normal and thats what our friendship is about.

its about the chalks, the blade and the nose of that snowman, its about things and memories we stored selfishly away for ourselves, basking in how really nothing, but a smile - is all that matters, at the end of the day.

Because of You

you bite my lip like its a part of you that you can't afford to lose, tickling my feet at night and asking me about the bad dreams that i have. i don't know if this is love but this is something, isn't it? the tickles and the lip bite, the confessions of bad dreams. i clutch the plastic bottle to my chest like it'll cure all the bruises i have on my skin but then one night you touch me and its like skin with bruises which are always capable of healing is all this is really about. the scars that show bravery, strength - the very marks of the fight i fought - you said

because of you - i murmur.

My Voice

Food Hurts

is it just a battle for me?

are the knives only scary for me?

is the steam coming off the dishes only choking me?

i wish it wasn't a joke or a big laugh when someone over ate a couple of calories, or if someone's clothes don't fit them any more

i wish the weighing scale would stop running behind me,

chasing and pulling into a circle of tapes that have a lot of numbers on it

no, no

dark brown cubes melt in my fingers and i don't remember putting my fingers in my mouth

my knuckles hurt undiscovered corners of my gums and my throat doesn't let me swallow

i feel a face somewhere in my mind smiling -

"this is you," it whispers

gone

all

gone

its just 3 seconds and its all gone,

looking around, the wrapped torn papers of the chocolate

i look in the mirror

i shouldn't have

the abuse

i look at the abuse on my hands and my mouth

my red rimmed eyes and my running nose

i can't think of where my saliva ends and my sweat begins

all i can think of is

is,

is the shame

i wipe the excess chocolate, brush down my hair, lick off the dark spots from my gums and wipe my face with the back of my hand and look again

i look in the mirror

i shouldn't have

i don't see the abuse

but i see me, i see *the me* in school and classrooms,

in front of my friends and neighbours

i see *the me* i rehearse so well

i know if you squeeze your eyes a little more,

dig in a little deeper,

come in a little closer,

you can see

you can see the well decorated abuse

but no one looks deeper

no one comes closer

do they?

The Pain Was Too Much

i'd promised myself - this was a line i'd never cross. this was a point i wasn't supposed to reach.

    the pain was so much, though

    it was beyond mental physical or emotional

    it was in my right vein and my left toe

    my forehead and my ears

    my tongue and the dripping saliva off the corner of my mouth

    i sat waist below naked in the corner

    the cold tiles stick against my thigh

    its been two hours - my sweat slicked thighs tell me

    i'm still breathing - and i owe it to the soft melody of a snore that i can hear from across the door

    my mother deep in slumber, and i pray, dreaming a dream full of pride for her child

    i smile as i think of her - and i send out a silent thank you. i don't know to whom, but i do.

    the pain was so much, though

now it reaches the pit of my stomach, the back of my head

i close my eyes to stop, control or maybe save myself

and i see - i see red blood in my body turning into an ugly green dark liquid

i test the sense of that liquid against my very layers of skin

its acidic.

i rub my palms against my mouth,

wiping off the saliva drooling down my throat

i rub my palms against my eyes and cheeks

closing my eyes - only to feel red ants crawling on the edges and biting their way into my skin

the pain was so, so, so much, though

and now its funny. it feels funny. its funny. funny's good. funny's okay. funny's not depressed. funny's not painful - i tell myself.

i sob and snort at the feel of the blunt sharpness of the blade

and i repeat - i'd promised myself - this was a line i'd never cross. this was a point i wasn't supposed to reach.

but i guess i could be forgiven - for in that moment - i would look at you funny and run away if you so as just asked me my name,

i whispered,

"i promise, i won't cut. i promise, i won't cut. i promise, i won't cut. i'm just trying to protect myself, from myself, in myself. i promise, i won't cut. the blade just feels funny. funny's good. funny's not painful. funny. funny. funny,"

the dripping sweat on crease of the outer thigh and the back of my knees tell me its been four hours,

i feel wetness between my legs, its thick, its sliding, and it feels funny

i sob and snort

i look down and cheat myself

i tell myself its red paint.

yes, paint.

'a 9 month heavily pregnant woman palming her swollen tummy and choosing to converse with the world within her body' - the last painting i made three months ago,

i look down and cheat myself again. yes, its red paint.

what would my father think? i told him i was okay at the breakfast table.

what would my mom think? i told her i didn't purge anymore.

what would my friends think? i told them it's not a big deal.

i giggle to myself, cry more, my lips feel twice their size between my teeth and my eyes are alert

the site between my legs looks painful but oh,

oh - funny. the funny feeling is so beautiful. there's no pain.

this is so beautiful.

i giggle myself and,

"shhh, it will always be our little secret," i tell my inner thighs.

i rub a sweaty palm across the cut, the red liquid, my skin, my trembling inner thighs

"i'm sorry," i whisper to my body - "the pain was too much."

Fooled memory

the plain white canvas laid emptied and abandoned in the centre of the living room. the room glowed with darkness and frustrated huffs of failure, of not being able to paint, of back to back senseless mess ups. there was silence but my head drummed an unbearable bass and sweat-slicked palms across my forehead only teased the anger more and more with each tick of the clock.

i felt a touch right then, i reckon. a pressure,

no, no

a pair of pale hands i wanted to push away but didn't because it was my medicinal touch. you hands were, are, and will always be the touch the hair on my skin choose to respond to. your hands, the only touch that forces my thighs to squeeze a little tighter, my breath to hitch a little more mightier.

you were always,

always,

always a devil,

but i couldn't bear the idea of saying no to it.

i closed my eyes and laid back, too tired to speak or protest, too tired to even exist. i slumped against the arm chair of the maroon couch which was itself an inanimate album of my warmest of memories with him. the snug pair of hands moved from my shoulders to my forearms and to my abdomen, encircling around my waist and locking me in a circuit of comfort and well, *home*. my thigh fit against his thigh almost like belonging pieces of a puzzle and i let out a hard sniff i didn't know i was holding back.

it was too much.

the hug felt too real, and that is what pained the most. it tugged my heart in all wrong ways until i started trembling again

i really wish i could hug back

before opening my eyes, i allowed himself a moment of a well scripted belief.

to imagine the hands to be real, to imagine the body on my lap real, to *let* it all be real. even if its only for a second.

i inhale and fool my nostrils into remembering the scent from exactly 7 years ago. *oh… its warm melted honey and natural sweet milk*

i drop my head imagining a hard rock shoulder to catch it, well built muscles radiating an unnerving softness, i nudged my cheek and imagine a rough beard against it, i slump my body and imagine a mediated masculine body to settle in the rhythm, like it always did.

does.

second's gone.

i open my droopy eyelids heavy with an emotion i can't put a name to. my breath hitches a noticeable peak as i stare into the darkness in front of me

its black. there's nothing.

i can see the shiny tinted glass of the kitchen door and my abandoned trousers on the floor, i can see my cat pet snoring too quietly in the lonely silence of the room, and i can see the uneven trail of pictures across the wall.

one particular frame with brown rusted boarders stores a memory that my heart and body lives to.

that frame shouts the words - *firmly planted roots.*

i can see the face in the stilled memory staring back, with an impromptu smile sprawled across that face with heavy black beard and a faint dimple on the right cheek, i can see the bushy eye brows furrowed in a happy frown and the adolescent crinkle of his nose. i can see the waves of brown hair fanning across his forehead as he plays blithely with my cat in the frame.

i can almost hear the dissolved laughter blooming from the frame and the unkind corners of my room.

i closed my eyes to replay the memory.

the colour of the grass and the bright mixture of lights ventilating from the sky, the breeze and coldness around the lake and the abandoned pieces of bread crumbs in the corner of the wooden chair. the torn sides of the picnic cloth and over stuffed basket. i think i can still smell the tempting hints of blueberry muffin.

i remember kissing.

kissing a lot.

so much so, that i almost remember him whispering in the most humorous way, "*i think we have traumatised your cat,*"

i remember jerking my head and looking at my cat, who blinked once, twice, and scratched the scalp of my head before running away from her crazy human.

i remember taking random pictures too. i remember holding hands in uncomfortable positions because it felt too wrong to let go, i remember having wine with ice cubes in plastic cups, watching the sun go down in all hues of undeniably beautiful colours from a sharp orange to a dull yellow to a dark blue and a plain hollow black with stars. i remember feeling his presence and gulping his warm vibes, his skin jovially as smooth as a buttery orgasm.

i remember forgetting everything and shrivelling my way into non existence with him as the evening came to an end.

a literal end.

and i've forgiven him. i really have. but i think in that whole process of letting him go and forgiving him so that he could move on with inner peace, i somewhere around *forgot to forgive myself.*

and maybe i won't ever be able to forgive myself for that.

i opened my eyes and faltered for a moment for i couldn't evaluate my own emotions or expressions or gestures.

i just felt a smile on my lips, a really really wide smile, and i felt a travelling wetness against my dry cheeks. what name would you give to this emotion?

i'm no human, darling

i'm a *mayhem of emotions.*

and i don't know where it goes from here. i wish i did.

Shell

i'll ask you to stay in your shell,

they want you to talk loud and be more energetic but i'm still gonna ask you to stay in your shell and talk about the things you love with the people who love to hear you talk, or that one quiet girl way back in the room in the corner who didn't kill herself because your quiet voice taught her that there are hundreds of boats like hers drowning in the same storm.

your quiet voice saved a life. *your shell's not only a home to you.*

Bulimia

you always like your salad hot and coffee cold on christmas evenings

but things have got sad off late. you got sad. you got bulimia.

and you made mirrors your enemy. you stopped wearing grey and dark blue and all your other favourite colours. you looked down upon every piece of skin. you got really sad, my love.

you stopped wearing the dress i fell in love with you in,

you whispered all the *shiny dirt* into my ears when i begged, really begged

"you feel punished. you vomit, and you feel like vomit for ages later. the feeling doesn't go. its not used to departures but only arrivals. the nausea is murderous like grammatical errors for poets. clothes become faces, teasing and laughing, itching and spitting. clothing stores start having jail bars and the watchmen looked at my waist all funny. i hold the bunch of skin near my outer thigh and it turns into sand, slipping out of my fingertips and laughing on the ground,

do i hear me

i'm scared. my body is turning into a monster. how do you keep your lips on it, still?"

i'll tell you - you're honey,

warm, gooey, melting, soft

you're satin,

soft, slippery, salty, satanic,

you're chocolate

firm, therapeutic, exquisite

you're a million priceless pieces of diamond and white little fairies

you're fire, my love, you're fire

you're the matchstick that never stops burning, immune to water and immune to sand

but you got sad,

you got bulimia and you got sad,

and i'll tell you my love the former doesn't matter

your sadness reminds me though — of broken wine bottles and you know how much i hate those,

you're much more than clothes and jails bars, mannequins and weighing machines,

you're a soul with powers of magic and i forever want to be one of your precious magic tricks.

you're still you

you're not your bulimia

i want to tell you our weakness isn't you. nausea shall leave some day, and that day i'll be right here with a jar of Nutella and a bucket of popcorns to hog onto with you, hold you and watch rerun of friends with you. i'll be right here my love. i want to tell you clothes don't matter really, and nakedness is beautiful. you're beautiful anyway as long as you have ink stains on your fingers with your bum on your childhood old desk, and fascinating ideas in your mind to write your fifth bestseller.

you know you hate the outside world but i'll tell you there isn't one,

there is only the lake we love to swim in all naked and raw and the cafe you sit in while you are on your typewriter. i'll tell you in that moment that only your fingertips matter even when they go through wild pieces of my hair.

so love, you see,

there is no outside world.

there's just the lake, the cafe, your typewriter, a few strands of my hair, and us,

and nothing like bulimia.

Hearts

i want to write so much, i think it should be almost scary for the words or the letters for the way they might be used.

i sing on sea depots at 12 am with a violin in my hand about my long lost love. but i'll tell you a secret, i don't know how to play a violin. this is a scene i'm enacting from this movie, where a girl goes by the sea shore in a bland peach beach dress, a see through exposing her beautiful body, and she plays violin for hours on end, endlessly for the love she just lost, almost celebrating her heartbreak,

i just got my heart broken. and i wish, i wish i could celebrate that like her too. i wish people celebrated death, or losing job, or a heartbreak. because isn't that life too? isn't death about life? isn't heartbreak about life? isn't losing a job about life? i wish people celebrated life more.

my heart holds so much it hurts, and sometimes i pray if heart had a language of its own, like braille for blind. a language only hearts understand. so before you meet a person, the hearts have talked. the hearts have made love. imagine, if hearts had a soul of their own. if hearts had an existence of their own. if they cried and weeped like us, if they breathed in and out like us. human mouths would say what the heart wants, human mind would do what the heart wants.

the hearts would make people live.

Candles

you light candles when you're sad and i wonder if thats your way of seeking some warmth and luminosity

you put your fingers to the burning nib until the small flame holes out and your finger comes back a little burnt and i wonder if that's your way to outrun the pain that's already in your chest

you light the flame again and inhale the scent of it and i wonder if that's a smell you've been chasing all this while

you look up and catch me staring with awe at the intimacy you share with a pile of wax and i don't say a word but just tell you that dinner's ready and there's choco chip pancakes for dessert.

you thank me with a million kisses and hugs like stars and sculpted mountains

later,

much later

after the dinner has been eaten and every small bit of pancakes has been gulped in with dishes all washed and dried near the sink, in front of the tv laid lazily across the couch which is just another irreplaceable part of them - they link fingers in the dark and refuse to look at each other his fingers nudge that sensitive spot behind her ear and the latter can't help but lean into the touch and purr like a kitten,

"hey, remember primary school? hiding under the benches away from those bullies? colouring flames of candles instead of superman and fairies?"

"no," she responds stubbornly,

"you remember, don't you?"

and sometimes you think there are bits of another person you can't touch and that should scare you but you don't realise that sometimes the person you love just lets you stand near those bits that they were unable to open up to the world and let you watch them unfold and grow in the most raw and scary manner

"yeah," she whispers,

"yeah." he whispers right back.

Irony of Life

its the ironical circle of life

a simple ID card - with name, age, birth date, home address.. all the basic details

a slight reminder of dependency

of vulnerability

a 3 year old cries as the stranger looks at his ID card and walks him to his home

he cries through the journey

oblivious and scared

prepared for the worst

and silently praying to be saved

the destination of the journey is a safe place, but he doesn't know

and he cries, cries, cries through the journey,

because this world is cruel, isn't it?

he's four, and oblivious. and scared. he needs a hand to guide him. his ID card apparently the only thing that saved him. a small piece of cardboard with a jumbled mess of letters that apparently saved him.

he went to school and didn't need the ID card anymore. he knew his name. he knew the places he had to go to.

years pass and he knew the name of his wife. his kids. he played with his grand-children. he signed cheques and danced in parties. he directed random lost strangers and tourists on the road. he was found and knew how to be found.

he's 83 now, with a simple ID card hanging off his shirt - all over again - its his favourite shirt and a simple act of love bestowed by his wife - but he doesn't know

a pair of eyes stare at him, they radiate a positive emotion - what, he doesn't know

he's walking down the road now, the left part of his body hurts, and there's a hammer hammering his skull, he doesn't know what to call this discomfort - he doesn't know what pain is - he doesn't know what a word is - he just feels it - and he doesn't even know that he feels it - he can't remember a thing

a voice gathers his attention. the human is talking.

the 83 year old man entranced by the movement of his lips, and the odd trance of sound coming from the stranger's mouth.

the stranger holds his hand, looks at the ID card on his shirt and guides him down the street to that house.

its the same - all eighty three years later.

he feels something familiar. its deja vu. its the same road. its the same number of steps. its the same destination - but he doesn't know.

thats the irony of life - *he doesn't know anything anymore.*

sketch3.jpg

People Laugh to Make You Laugh

friends

its not the person sometimes. its more like their laughter that you miss.

i'm not talking about missing really. i'm talking about emptiness.

you were with them and suddenly them are gone home. because people have homes to go to, they have lives to live, people to meet, loves to love. they leave and with their departure there's an echo of laughter that radiates off walls, you think of their smiles in an old fashioned way as if they were dead. but they're alive and you meet them. but you just miss them.

your heart feels full like a bucket of water, or a ship that's about to sink. because you realise its not missing. its absence. and absence feels more like being incomplete. and when you're incomplete. you're sinking an inevitable sink. and then you realise how needy you are.

you miss their laughter and their funny dances, their aura of making everything okay, their talks of old school memories about short skirts and the girl with heavy breasts, you miss their voice too, like a lullaby. and mostly you miss their soul. yes, their very soul. the soul you hug when they enter your house and offer you warmest of hugs after days of being away, the soul that meets and discusses life happenings over a glass of wine or a cup of coffee, the soul that stays together no matter how away you are. so close and intertwined that more of closeness is not humanly possible.

you think of balloons and clowns and you laugh then with tears in your eyes because you've been a sad girl. a very sad girl. you've cried day and nights and its been a tough battle but they make it better. they always do and the best part is they always will. you've hurt so much that normalcy feels anew and, and maybe scary too. but with them its just… its just okay. there's no normalcy and there's no fear. you are just you, a mixture of misery and recovery. and they are them in the most beautiful and pure way - like a bunch of laughters here to echo until it becomes the laughter coming out of your mouth. they'll laugh until you laugh, until the tears in your eyes vanish and until the ache kind of subsides for a while. they laugh to make you laugh.

and i ask you, do you have people who laugh for you with pain in their hearts and lives? do you have people that laugh, just to make you laugh?

i do.

Like its All About Sundays

he folds newspaper cuttings and uses them to wipe things,

the foam of his toothpaste or his shaving cream,

extra glue off his paperwork or fallen ash on the dinner table,

sometimes the corner of his mouth too

its about Sundays, really

he folds the old dated newspapers cleaner and sharper,

like - like -

like they matter, you know?

like small things matter. remembering a date or remembering your father's favourite kind of flower,

or keeping that old dress even if it doesn't fit you or that blank piece of paper with nothings just for the sake of it,

like they really matter, you know?

its all about Sundays, really

he'd fold them neat and cut them raw with his knife,

his wifebeater with 3 holes just another small thing that really matters, or the ink on either of his collarbones, behind his earlobe and centre of his navel,

he has coffee at exactly 3 am every morning and there isn't a fault in his motorcycle he can't fix,

like - like -

his hands have magic, you know?

and i see the magic too - maybe not sparkles or shiny lines, or beatified perfected nails and smooth skin

but magic more like the cuts from being careful with old newspapers and aura of petroleum and metal his fingers and palm radiates

its magic - watching him exist,

sat across me folding newspapers and cutting them neat for the day on Sundays

not smiling but still looking at me every few minutes like he knows i'm there

like i'm another one of his small things,

small things,

like i really matter,

like its all about Sundays, really

and its magic - when i smile because he doesn't and the next few cut pieces of newspaper by his hands are sharper, cleaner, and crisper than the last few

its magic

its all about Sundays, really

My Own Demon and Beast

did you know?
    i'm not really that brave
    one pill or a whole bottle sometimes
    drunk on unhealthy things unlike alcohol
    smile on things like failure
    and sometimes pain.
    what am i? my own beast? my own demon?
    the mirrors are the same in all kind of countries,
    cruel, negative, rude, bullying — i think
    just real — they say
    i set rules i want to break
    only to feel more pathetic
    i break the rules that don't exist
    only to make it worse
    what am i? my own beast? my own demon?
    "demons have black wings, and you're sweetness, my love,"

mum whispered

i shake my head from the ceiling to the ground

yes - i say

"i have wings too, mum

i have wings too

they look white to you

but they feel so — black

they itch and tease my skin

but, they look so white to the world and you,

and i see the way you smile, mum

when you see that whiteness too."

so, yes - i say

always keep my mum smiling, i pray

but did you know?

i'm not really that brave

what am i? my own demon? my own beast?

i'd walk away and apologise to things like chocolates, gifts and nice pretty sweets

door

the brown door

i'd smile on one side

cry and wail my lungs out the other

i'd scratch and punch the wood with the company of the moon

and hide my sins with the company of the sun

"the scratches are creepy," my friend states

"its just a brown door," i whisper

so yes - say

always keep mum smiling, i pray

but now you know

i'm not really that brave

i am, my own demon

i am, my own beast

The Boy With the Scariest Scar

and probably after all these years of breathing, this was the first time i wanted to remove it and just be without it

he turned his face toward the window, looking out as if the carefree bird etching homes and songs onto the bask of the dark tree would come save him,

the touch of the heat of the sun waved his face and the large bandage on his cheek into hues of oranges and golden and just so shiny,

it was the brightest sadness i'd seen etched onto someone's skin and bones

his fingers traced the edge of the bandage and his eyes bore holes into mine. holes asking for permission, for validation. the glue lines stuck and slid until the whole white piece of a bandage full of abuse came off.

i felt nothing. my heart didn't shift ten steps nor did i want to flinch. the scar was darker on some binds and lighter than his original skin. i thought they were just another two beautiful shades of his caramel skin.

they looked a lot like pain, *weeping in a corner of a wooden house with a pool of blood.*

the scar was so brave.

i inched forward, the holes in our eyes connected and yoked, letting him know i was on my way. i cupped his other cheek and a smile etched onto my lips when his eyes fought some wetness. i traced the scar with my fingers, my blunt nails boring small pressures into the skin and saying something like brave and you're loved and i've got a whole new home waiting for you,

i touched our foreheads and closed my eyes to inhale his hidden hiccups. the smile wouldn't leave my lips, for it was kind of radiating off my insides which were just so full and swollen with pride and fond for this utterly brave boy i love, who survived knives and bruises,

i started from the other side of his face, stroking each invisible line and pore of his skin, from his jaw to his cheekbone, his right flurry eyebrow and small bits of standing hair near his ear, his forehead slicked with salty sweat tasting like prosperity - and reaching the other side, the untouched one, i stopped kissing and placed my nose right beside his, sniffing in his existence and trying to trade some calmness, i inhaled the smell of insulted skin and moved the perk of my lips, tracing each small dent, curb, and line with all the love my lips could hold - i tasted so much of sadness that i wanted to cry, my eyes were closed and i got visions of a boy weeping and crying to sleep, shivering in pain, bullied for a brave scar, and i wanted to tell him how sad it makes me that he left his scar so unloved and suffered.

i wasn't surprised when i heard familiar mewls, making me smile - he wasn't holding back. and for the first time i felt like i could actually hold him all - for what he is, for what he's suffered and gone through - and love him, love him so much for the things he never was and love him for being just born.

"i could get hopelessly drunk on that scar," i whispered, with fondness cascading from my hands cupping his cheek, and the peck of my lips quivering with his lashes.

i don't remember it all for it was all blurs after that. all i can think of is now.

sitting beneath the big oak tree we grew around and shared our first kiss, and spilled secrets about scars - murdering scars. and also where we healed, together, where we grew, together - for ourselves and for each other. my fingers drew ransomed practiced patterns with ease on his scar and his face inched a step closer in my lap, i looked at his skin, the old pink converse he wore, the sweat pooling on the dent of his collarbone and his warm breath fanning against my jumper, and then i looked at him.

the boy with the scariest looked healed.

Grandfather

my grandfather played board games when he got bored

with a long white beard and wrinkles on his face like dances on a stage

his home smelled like old butter biscuits and warm old Indian tea

a lot of oil and some ecstatic desert

and then that time as a teenager

i was lost in rebel

a little too gone to really count on the board games and the butter

but he did what he'd always do

take a drive to the places he loves wearing a fifty year old gold wedding ring

a shiny, expensive ring

but his own shine outshone the gold every time i looked at him

because he lived - which not everybody does

the skeletons all free from his closet and free of bounds

he lived

for fires in winter

and the cool air in summer

for small family moments and magics of nature

and when i think of him

i think of rainbow lollipops and a dark sky with a hope of rain — i think of soul and the wonder of enjoying life

the white drizzle of snow and sparkle of a christmas tree star

i think of life and to live

to live

what you are

what you have

and what you need

to live every aspect of your life because time runs out like sand in hand

and you'll be stood too lost a rebel in your own lonely land

My Tears

the now

i wish you'd look at the other side of the pillow a little more deeply,

and when you'd ask me what's wrong in my numb moments, my voice giving up on me,

i wish you'd understand that my eyes try to talk, they answer your questions

you never really get away with self harm, you just really learn to do it ways that don't leave scars

the pillow's a little damp but you think that's water. i feel shame. not on myself. but you. i feel its shame on you. That's not water. That's my tears. don't you smell it? its misery and pain, so much pain. its unforgivable threats and abuses. its liquidated scars. my scars.

you trace the mark on the stain and ask me to get it washed.

and a part of me feels shame again

not on you

but myself

for serving my soul in the hands of a murderer like you

a murderer that knows no tears

how do you marry a man who knows no tears?

the before

but

but *once upon a time, he was this stranger at the airport. he hid behind visas and tickets. his face looked like a mayhem of sickness and i wanted to ask if there's something i can do to make things better. i was with my mom because crowds scare, and i squeezed her hands a degree tighter because i'm not used to beautiful sights.*

the stranger squished his eyes and there were bundles of skin under and above his eyes, he looked at least 15 years elder to me and i felt sad. sad because its unfair to like someone and not have a chance. not have a chance of even having a chance. there was anxiety in my veins and places like airports always reminded me of snowstorms anyway.

but god blessed me.

i opened the door to the sitting door looking down because that's how i am, with my cup of hot chocolate foaming in my hold and he was right there. he was just right there

the after

i don't know how your presence feels no more but i'm hoping so much.

i'm hoping that you've finally found the courage to be you, to follow your desires and ask the girl of your dreams to be yours for years and years to come. i hope your parents are good, i miss them when all dorm kids go out on Sundays with their families for lunches and dinners and wine games. i'm hoping for you even when i see pretty summer clothes for they remind me on that time in summer on the beaches with your pretty little nieces, yellow sunbathing suits with bottles of lemonades, brown bread sandwiches with extra extra, and extra cheese.

and i don't know if this very voice reaches you but i also think that's not the point, every day as i wake up to face days, clocks and human walks, i shall take a second to hope for you — and i think its okay, its okay if i chose to fall out of love.

He Read to Me

you read to me all the time. in tubs when we bathed, skin to skin and atom to atom, lips on collarbones and a hand inside me

i keep a foot on your shoulder and command

"you first read to me

then

then, we make love,"

it would be stories of empresses' that ran away for true love, books of superheroes saving the world, novels of lovers uniting after ages and a play about a woman dying.

with him i live

i'd live a new life

a new story every day

every second a new word

every millisecond a new alphabet

he spoke a thousand languages - i think when i look at his eyes moving, ears twitching, chin lifting, lips puckering, lashes fluttering i tell him this every day

that my favourite out of the thousand

is the language of your collarbone

the right collarbone, one with the ink

and a scar when you fell as a fiver

a mole so beautiful

and your breath uneven

the language of your collarbone would tell me how, for you, the things considered ugly by people, were beautiful

your nipples would erect out of shyness and i'd tell you it's okay, love, it's okay, let's go on a cycling trip for a weekend, to a land without a name with air that doesn't know us, let's go to a new cottage, living a new story, a new life, for outside the doors of my wooden house, there's not one but millions to call love between a number 18 and 29, a game of lust,

your fingers firmly hold the base of the book, and kissing my naked hip you'd say the lines of a character i am falling in love with. i look at the alphabets and fall in love with the curve of alphabet 'a' on your collarbone, and the border of the book is like the scar and i think,

i think you're the book out of all books. you're the book that changes lives and offers alternative gash of air, you're the book people hold onto for hope and search the words in need of answers. you're the book that reads me thousands of letters and lines, fascinating me with the movement of your lips and fingers, the sigh off your pink mouth and butter sliding off your lower lip.

you're the book that uses rose petals for book marks, and i think — i think i'm in love with my favourite book, that reads to me every single day.

Coming Back From My Own Kill

this is me coming back from my own kill.

i remember blades like a blurred vision and papers torn on the carpet floor. tissues. loads of tissues. i remember wiping my skin and damaged muscles because hush, i gotta be quiet, i can't let my secret out.

what would the neighbours think?

i remember a few drops of blood falling on the ground.

"crap, you're a piece of crap."

walking like a zombie into the wall. and darkness. my shorts falling off my waist and making me naked thigh below. i'm a boy. i was wearing a bra. my hands super cold from the trauma. i bathed for 2 hours. an hour i did something i'm not proud of. an hour, i cried. i think you're allowed crying. i think they forgive you for crying in the church.

i think so because crying doesn't leave a scar.

i open my eyes and see familiar faces asking me if i'm okay. i'm not. they know. my head lolling from my side to side like a beautiful release technique. classes. i wish i could play my music right now. i wish i wasn't hurting. i wish the sting of pain on my fingertips were the strings of a guitar instead of blade. i wish i was sensible. i see my heartbeat on a human made machine. how fascinating is that? there's a bright light above me and it hurts my eyes. but i wonder if anyone ever said that to these partial blue beings slinging things into my body, from tubes to needles to cotton to, oh yes, music. i dream of music. i played my favourite tune earlier this morning and i'd got it right and didn't tell anyone about it. i had been trying to get it right for quite a while now. i wish i had told someone.

i see faces of my friends crying and my parents weeping.

it doesn't make sense to me.

once upon a time, there was a boy that didn't belong.

nursery, pushed away from the carpet, primary, locked into the girls' washroom - to high school, pushed against the painful lockers,

i wish, with this bright light in front of my face and a type of human breed like doctors around me, i wish i could speak up. speak up about things like that not being as funny as they seem. the laughs that follow not as worth as someone's life or someone's self esteem.

i wonder if i had spoken up, would people have a place in this world for the kind that don't belong? the kind that loves music but refuses to follow the music industry and loves dancing but refuses to follow the dance industry? the kind that doesn't wish to follow or lead but only exist, exist for goodness and kindness because how many people can you name that decide to exist for goodness and kindness? zero. i think zero.

i open my eyes and don't see doctors no more. i see a silent room, the beep of some machine the only music i'm accustomed to listen to with the silence hollowing me. i don't mind. the beep and the silence seems to be off and away from the touch of humans and politics, and so, i don't mind.

i miss my box. i'm a boy, told more blue than pink.

my box has pink bows on it. i have a hidden collection of pink nail paint in it. it also has my old guitar string, the blade i cut myself with sometimes, my journal that i cry into. its a blank journal with tear stains.

i wonder people made journals for crying too. it would save lives.

that box has a polaroid image of my dad in his college days, all raw and young, his smile like my unhealthy heartbeat and his hands in a peace sign because i had a cool dad, he's smiling so big that the coldness of my toes takes a silent departure for a while upon that memory. my mom doesn't know i have that picture. she doesn't need to know. she shouldn't know. i want to live, so she shouldn't know.

i think of nights i cried, with pink nail paint and bows on my box, and the polaroid image drowned deep in my tears, i think if he had taken me with him far away from my mother, from her snow voice and from her punctured abuse.

i wouldn't have made blade my friends, if he had become mine.

i realise i'm alive. this is me coming back from my own kill. but i wish, i wish i was in a toilet right now. toilet lids greet me much happier than my mom does. slaps and knuckle hits aren't that warming, are they?

the blankness of this hospital room makes me feel like i'm dead. a feeling i was craving and probably chasing. i imagine red old England leaves and trees around myself. and my grandmothers' house's beautiful fence, it was white, curvy, and ancient. just like her. and it was homey, just like her. i wish my grandmother was holding my hand right now, the cut veins would hurt less, but then i think there's nothing that could reduce the pain, even after the surgeries and the bandages, because sometimes,

sometimes pain decided to grow from its roots in places that are unreachable.

its distant and hidden and just so apart, you can touch your soul, but you can't touch this pain.

this pain.

and this is why, i'm not sorry for who i am and what i do. i'm never sorry. i'm not sorry for blades or for cuts, for i was told pink is not my colour, for my dad decided i wasn't worth a handshake, for my mother decided that all i deserved, was love the size of a wounded slit.

sometimes i think if i could talk to the stars at night because it gets really lonely. and if i could write or sing forever without an artists' block because there's nothing else that saves me. i sit here thinking of words to type and sing and they don't come and that time i only see and think blood and harm. where did this much pain come from

Its Just Us Today

and its the faded sound of *"how many nights did it take to count the stars, that's the time it would take to fix my heart,"* with a slight buzz of the refrigerator in the background, the second pin of the clock ticking.

she likes things like that. small things that make their presence known in small ways, by a small sound or through a constant buzz, or like songs we imagine that play in the background in our lives at different points, thinking of words you could've said and the kisses you could've kissed.

"its just us today, it always has been,"

we've been playing liars. defying the gratification of love to each other over these years, and when we share coffee in the morning in between yawns, while i rub my belly and she puts her bra on, or like when she's sleeping right beside me and sniffles a movement a little and my hand reflexively goes to shush her and put her back to her dreams i reckon consist of me or even if they don't, i'm content with watching her smile because it looks like she's having a good dream.

we're been playing liars for so long and showing love in the way we *don't* do things for each other. like don't stand too close in front of each others' boyfriend or girlfriend or how still she calls me 'mate' and i let her and the way she licks the corner of the cup i take a sip from and i see it but don't tell and she sees me seeing her but she doesn't tell and we just don't tell.

we bare our hearts and lie to them on the face and sometimes i think whats the point. sometimes i think why live the lie? why not go for it?

the fear never goes away, does it?

the fear of losing our medicines to fix each others' heart, sipping coffee from the same cup and having stashed weed like its our dirty little secret and i wonder if some day you'll actually catch me feeding off the paint stuck under your nails like its art and tell me about it. because i hope one day you do.

that one day you catch me staring at you with something else in the way my palm skims over your backbone and your spinal knob and how i lick that side of the coffee cup right back.

and that one day, i'm hoping one day the fear will be replaced by a small flaw of courage by the both of us and while you would string your guitar to start of your gig, with cigarette in the other hand, i'm hoping i'll lean up and kiss you and i'm hoping that kiss would tell you *we're nothing like them* and *its just us and the way we've always been* and, and *how not a single thing about the yawns of our morning coffee would change.*

and *some day when we've permanently fought the fear i'd hope some time in a sixty we'd laugh off the memories of coffee and kisses and nights spent counting star and hugging each other for love but pretending otherwise and i'm aware maybe the fear is what makes the kisses more exciting and the stares more worthwhile but i can't, with all my heart, wait for the day we'd like each others' mouths instead of the side of the coffee cup.*

His Silence

he didn't ask me about my 3 am thoughts

nor the things i am comfortable about

thats the thing

he didn't ask. he didn't talk. he just existed and waited for things to unfold. and it abashed me to find a man who so carelessly offers his life to the clever play of time and fate and the magic of unfurling

he didn't ask me about my kinks or my fetishes

but i think he saw them

he didn't ask me about the things that'd help me grown, or heal previous wounds

he did though, on this random Thursday ask me about my favourite book

i think he likes books

or maybe just pages with words on it

he asked me about my favourite book and favourite author

and the moment that caused the former

in that moment

i talked about the things i like in life

whether i prefer

a wild night in

or a quiet night out

whether i communicate

through body

or mouth

and some days he'd go hours without exchanging a single word and those times i realised before being mine he's his own. he's his own silence and calmness and then he's mine and i can never change that. it amazed me to see him live in his own skin. he earned 20 quid an hour and took buses to work but his smile after having the first sip of his mint tea wasn't even worth something like human made money.

and then on a February

i guess 12th or 28th

i realised its a shared silence

thats all there is

the shared silence with always our bodies drawing to each other like two separate bits meant to breathe in and out together and i don't think now i can ever go a day without living the silence with him,

silence of silent meals and silent love making or silent promises

he never said i love you

he never made promises

his silence did

he made me feel loved and kept un said promises and on those days i wondered about the exaggerated importance of words and syllables and felt foolish every time i opened my mouth to talk

the man functions like magic, selling his work worth 100 quid to a kid with a worn out skirt for 1 quid and a couple of chocolates to go with,

he moves like an act of kindness and i wonder if he's human

the man functions like magic

breathing in sand and breathing our sparkle

folding in the devil and giving birth to little angels

killing the words and making me fall in love with silence

taking in black and giving out white

i, his keel, and he, my kite

There's Always a New Home

where was he?

i really don't know where it all went wrong. i turned the lamp on and off. i played with the ring on my finger. the antagonism between my heart & my mind eliminating my peace bit by bit. my mind was being my own biggest enemy. sometimes i wish i had the power to turn off my thought process and be a dumb body that is just breathing to survive. the memories really do hurt.

i suppose sometimes its the best to let go. it did good, but it's not doing that anymore. you tried, but it doesn't work. you tell yourself you're pathetic for not being able to pull it off, but - some things just come to go, some things just come with a limited life span in your life. we tend to grow familiar with the idea of good things lasting till the very end. that is a pathetic concept. get over it. just because it did good to you once, doesn't mean it will do good to for the rest of your life. you have a heart that beats - so you'll just know when it's over. there's nothing more graceful and beautiful than letting go of the good things in your life happily when they actually need to go. be it a person you love, your job, your friend, your home, anything. letting go for good is a symbol of strength.

i blinked my eyes after what felt like ages. they sting.

6 am.

the time didn't stop, did it? the clock kept ticking. somewhere around i could hear him breathing a bunch of words into my mind.

"i'm not coming home tonight." we both were too scared to end it. so the time did, for us. and i stopped crying

and i went to sleep with a growing realisation that another beautiful home awaits me.

Some Days It Gets Harder

i think some days it gets harder than its supposed to be. the pain becomes unreal and your stomach hurts but its not actually your stomach, its your very soul. you look around the room to find the meaning of the existence of your cupboard or the mirror you got so happily or maybe you're trying to find the meaning of your own existence.

you promised you'd never do it again but thats the thing about addicts - their promises go as far as a plea of try and, — and thats all you should really expect. promises and addicts don't go together.

but that day,

that day you stopped -

and you tried to look at where it hurt. your leg? your thigh? your chest? where is the pain coming from?

you closed your eyes and the exhaustive ache came back to your lashes, your wet eyes dripped some more pain and you let out an inaudible sigh, you clenched the core of your stomach where there's no organ, no bones and you'd believe no blood too. you hold that point below your navel with all that you have. your leftover strength, your tolerance, and your pain too. you grunt out unfamiliar sounds and shout that its unfair to feel a pain thats not even there in the first place.

my mind, how powerful are you

you grunted all that you had

and hours later

you find myself half close to relief lying on the floor and your addiction lying a couple steps too far away.

its unused. the packet's sealed. still.

your right hand is splayed still and calm across your navel, shushing the left over pain.

"shhh, shhh," you beg, you whimper

"one day at a time." you say to the pain - "i promise to welcome you, take care of you, and shush you back to sleep every time you come, because.. because one day at a time,"

some times we think in life what really remarks glory is 'when we make it' or when we've achieved solace and contentment. but i'm gonna tell you this is a bunch of bullshit. remarkable glory and happiness *is about pain*, its about smiling through that ache in your stomach and finding love in the smallest of things, its about hugs you should bother with more and that moment of life you achieve in itself when you're allowed to open your eyes in the morning. if there's no pain, there would be no happiness. we're fools thinking they're wide apart, happiness and pain go in hand in hand, very much in love, to infinity and beyond with their own forever and we like fools think they're world apart and one has to be fought to achieve the other. no. bear the pain and be fucking happy if there's breath in your lungs. happiness isn't about smiles and laughter and calmness, happiness is about being okay with your existence, happiness can be even about being sad with tears brimming your eyes, happiness is accepting pain and not fighting it, its existing every day through highs and lows and not channeling an expiry date to your life. this is what remarkable happiness is, this is what real remarkable glory is.

Ancient

he kept his hand on my waist and pulled me close. closer. if any more closeness was possible. i looked away immediately. the intensity of what we have murders me every day.

his cufflinks rub against the small revealing part of my back bone and his metal rings clink in a melodious tone, and i wonder if he would sing right now because he's to me what melody's to the world. the metal ring doesn't go well with the prom suit. he doesn't go well with the world. supposed world.

its not how we moved

its the way we moved

its what made us move

i'd say affection

fond

warmth

a side alley replaces the prom hall and its all dark. the algae mewls off the windows of the old house windows on either sides and i smell 'oldness'. a smell you don't find all that often nowadays because everyone loves new. its a smell i live for.

that 'old' smell is his natural, every day

when i nub my nose into the space between his arm and ribcage

his armpits smell of old

his neck smells of old

old houses, old books, old blankets

and old love

its now how old smelled

its the way he made old smell

its what made him smell odd

i'd say ancient

gold eaten

unique

my prom dress is ruined and so are we. i remember a story my mother told me as a kid when i tried to believe that goodness exists, that best things are the hardest to keep, and you must fight for them. she forgot to tell it was this hard. that you have to fight with every drop of blood in your being, for and with your best thing. your best person. your person. your fond, warm, golden and unique person. who smells of old things. whose collarbone is your home and his rings are a vision you wish to wake up to every day, whose fingers you bite because he doesn't, whose anxiety you take because you care, whose smile you widen because it matters and whose love you wish to keep irrevocably because its oxygen. oxygen for you.

it was the inner chords of his heart that moved my feet and i wouldn't call this dancing. i think its more. much much more.

i rubbed my head between his armpit, silently sniffing and ended up with my head on the inside of his neck. i smell silently because the old smell and i, we're a secret he shouldn't know. there's some struggle to hold onto. because as hard it is to fight for and with your best things, its even harder to hold onto them for dear life.

i clutch my hands tight and leave hand prints on his back, decorated well with the teeth marks and the nail marks.

To Love a Wounded Heart

it took us a while.

3 long weeks of texting and precisely 9-10 coffee dates in infamous cafes across the town to get him to just hold my hand

its no secret, he couldn't take the touches. it was as if he despised anything mobile and with life. he barely spoke. but the very few syllables that left his mouth made much more sense than the constant blabber of other mouths.

and i cant help but swell with warmth realising that a boy with a wounded heart introduced me to the rare concept of emotional intimacy and the unknown angles of love i didn't know a thing about.

on the rarest of moments he held my hands, and on other days he just, just initiated that intimacy, it was in the way his fond showed when i made tea in the kitchen and he played with my cat, he was a star with a shine dulling its way into death and at the same time battling its way into sparkle

and every once in a while, he'd smile. the kind smiles that people don't give anymore.

and maybe it was also in the way he didn't lie when i asked him if he still misses her, or if it still aches every day,

to love him and his aching edges made me lose myself in a world only making me hope that i'm never found again.

and on some nights, i hid it all

i cried because his sadness did get to me too

i cried because it was painful

painful and worth it

and it baffled me sometimes. because it was a broken heart that did all this.

the kind smiles

the unquestionable honesty

the loyalty

sometimes i'm afraid i'd touch your chest while you're asleep and my hand would linger on blood smeared right across with your eyes wet from wretched ache in your bones. and that some day the tea would run cold on the kitchen table with you staring into space in a way that whispers a goodbye. i'm so afraid it breaks my heart but i also think, you use rocks for support to crawl and i? i fell in love with the way you crawl despite bits of blood and madness of humans shouting to pull you down.

He Breathed

he breathed chocolate into my mouth when i cried

    like the first bright of summer and first snow of winter

    he pasted sparkle at the edges of my teeth, forming a haze and tracing patterns with his tongue

    when our lips, all naked, touched a piece of each others' skin

    he'd look at me

    like i allowed him to breathe

    to breathe sin into my mouth

    he'd suck the bottom lip in apology of the sins

    and my tongue would say its okay by doing a little twirl

    and another

    and another

    my tongue would dance with his

    accepting his sins as my own

    he breathed lavender into my mouth on weekdays when i refused to go to work lavender to get me out of bed into the world of his being

his white see through shirt and manly arms

his walk and sin of a mouth

sin

he exists like a sin

secretive

a silent killer

he breathed loaded guns into my mouth

my tongue would joyously load the gun and pull the trigger with his

its funny the shot goes to my chest and not the back of my mouth

I Wish I Was Your Friend First

i wish we had talked. really talked. had become closer humans,

closer like veins and bones and the rhythm of the blood types

i wish our bodies had waited

our lips had halted that night

i wish i had asked you about the uneven lined up frames

the used band aids scattered across the kitchen counter

i wish i would've questioned the excess need to be close to someone

the constant reminder that you get off on absence of your loved ones

you get off on pain and heartbreaks and i wish i'd asked you more questions

stayed more nights talking in the company of tea mugs

i wish

i wish i'd tried

i wish i'd tried to get closer in more ways than one

closer in a way that shouts, danger

i wish i'd whispered the truths i felt but didn't have the courage to utter

that you're like graffiti on random streets

graffiti without names

full of art that tugs your heart

and holds you close even when you're a country apart

i look at the graffiti, the mixed paints, the artists who don't wanna be known, the melting of emotions down the brick walls, the portray of an abandoned kid and a mother left mid way, i think of the sunsets this wall faces, kisses, licks and mewls with. the love it makes to the passersby and the dances it watches of the first dates, like shining smiles and hugs tucked under your chin, your neck bared and love marks. so many marks like dances of red paint on the wall.

i think of abandoned wishes made in the aisle of a church, wishes they know won't come true, wishes made for the sake of wishing, for the sake feeling the sense of those words against the coil of your lips. i think of folding your arms in front of your chest even though you don't carry a belief in your heart but today you need to be saved and its alright to think maybe someone is really out there, someone looking out for you. i think of hot pleading breath against the flat of your palm, begging, whimpering sounds radiating off my throat, pleads of maybe love is not enough. maybe there actually is more to love that just love. maybe, maybe its friendship is all that love really is.

i look at the graffiti and i think *you.*

and i think of that moment where i wished i was more than just a mere mistletoe kiss

i wish

i wish i could be your friend.

I Wish You'd Given Our Childhood a Chance

i remember you. i remember us at four.

i remember mud pies and cracks of nails full of dirt, the threads dangling from the end of my socks and your slipping suspenders. running around the backyards of our houses and making a joint home somewhere between the adjoining railing of two distant properties. a home stood on a rough bark of a tree and white see through cloth.

i remember feeling what home is before knowing the word 'home' itself with you.

i remember you. i remember us at nine.

and i still remember our very first home with that white see through cloth. its dirtier now but there's something about the smell of it that stops us for changing it and bringing in a brighter white cloth. we like the dull. or more, we like the dull together. reflecting off the dancing shadows of the sun on our skin through the cloth, your hand covering the hollow of my eyes to dull the sharp sting of the light.

i remember sniffing the sweat of your hand and thinking - home.

i remember you. i remember us at fourteen.

and i still remember our very first home. the white cloth has holes in it, and there are strings off bits and pieces of it from the corner. it looks rotten and old - it looks like us, i remember going there on good days and bad days. on days you want to tell me about the first kiss of your life and on days i nag to you about my very first period.

i remember looking at it trying to see my childhood and seeing your face with a mushroom cut and slipping suspenders.

i remember you. i remember us at 19.

i remember sitting in the home we made as kids and watching through the hole the pretty blonde girl you help walk into your house. i watch her hug your mom and my skin afire. i remember looking up after wiping my nose with the back of your jumper and looking right in the eyes of your mother. she knew. she always knew. her eyes tell me her son's a fool and mine tell her he's anything but.

your son's my star, did you know?

i remember you. i remember us at 24.

the white cloth is all grey and light brown and it looks like my favourite piece of painting. we still sat there sometimes after i returned from my gallery and you returned from your music studio. i remember holding your hand on bad days and listening to different rhythms with the taps of your fingers and the blink of your eyes. i remember some nights you'd hold me different and let me fall asleep on you. my face dug deep into your stomach and my breast perfectly sculpted into your thighs. i'd pretend to be asleep to see the way you are around the oblivious me.

you're raw. you take deep breaths once i'm fast asleep and you caress the back of my neck with your first two fingers, you reach near the zipper of my dress and you stop. you always stop. you'd squeeze my head tighter and sometimes hold me like there's nothing else in the world that matters. you'd rub the nub of my worn out fingers and almost kiss the paint dented nails. something my boyfriend never does.

and after the almost kiss i'd whine and snort a step or two closer into your navel, sniffing off the strong smell of your existence from the gap between your t shirt and your boxers. something your girlfriend never does.

on days like that i wish the sun would never come up.

i remember you. i remember us at 29.

i remember confessions of love and how weird it feels. how right it feels but how wrong it seems.

i remember watching you give up because tour buses and art galleries aren't backyards with our white cloth of a tent and our safe house, they are not the barbies we played with and the mud pies you made. life's not our white cloth of a tent.

i remember slapping you. because life could be anything you want it to be. i remember wishing you'd given me a chance.

and i remember sleeping alone in our white cloth of a tent for the very first time, wishing with every ant crossing my way, for our 'home' to crumble into trash when i wake up.

i remember you. i remember us at 35.

we don't come in our white home any more.

but today i look at you at the dinner table, zoning out the catching up of our families and friends, you won't look at me, you won't acknowledge me. you just won't see me in the face. your wife would hug me and kiss me on the cheek and you'd look at my skin with hungry eyes. my husband would shake hands with you and your handshake would look more like a punch to his balls.

your eyes and hands, and your presence reminds me of a white something and i can't help but hook my ankle with yours under the table.

i look at you checking up on our legal soul mates only to find them engrossed with our families. you take my hand and lead us to our backyard, where our houses join, where our home existed.

exists.

i barely see the cloth anymore. its gone in the winds and its bits must rest in peace in crumbs in the wet mud. i somehow am fond and proud of the way it chose to vanish, of the way it chose to not die but to just go on till the very end, till the very last thread. i am proud of how it chose to not die but rather vanish with its bits and pieces still grounded deep in the roots of the yards.

but i can still see the stones you stuck in the mud, the round shaped one, and the fancy boxes you adored and got to show me. i could see miniature cars and small barbie accessories lost and abandoned in corners but still there.

our hands still interlocked and you avoiding my gaze, i see you stare at it all. wishing,

just wishing,

and i squeeze your hand tighter because i wish the same,

i wish you'd given our childhood a chance.

Fell for a Boy Not Allowed to Fall For

i wasn't allowed to fall in love with him,

it's this boy that lives down the street. he's not well off and lives without his parents. my dad asks me to stay away from him, his ash tray and second hand guitar a bit too intimidating, his beard is a beautiful croissant of black and brown, making me wonder what he smells like.

and his skin tone reminds me of lavender and the feel of its petals and the sense of stems reminds me of the way people see him. how my dad sees him.

how i'm confined to see him.

there would be smoke in his eyes and softness in the way he looks at the world every time

like the kind devil,

i'd cross his house on our street holding my dad's hand. i'd look at him in disgust, the way i'm conditioned to look at him,

but he looked at me right through my spirit, right through me, right through the way i'm asked to perceive him. his cigarettes would tilt hanging off his lips and he'd smile a smile like he knows the act i put up. like it's not a secret that he's a big part of my dreams and my showers. like a big part of me,

there are rat holes outside his house, rat holes he takes care of, and rats he feeds, rats that my dad kicks and scoffs at.

i like rats.

it's about this boy that lives down the street. he's not well off and lives without his parents. my dad asks me to stay away from him, his ash tray and second hand guitar a bit too intimidating.

and his beard

his beard is a world, which on some days i can't wait to explore although he's 6 years elder to me. black with small borders of dark brown, like a master piece of a painting or a texture you look at and cry because it's so damn beautiful.

you'd see the cigarette dangling from his lips for endless minutes and his throat humming a tune along his fingers on the guitar and i wish, i wish someone would tell him he's beautiful,

that his appearance doesn't deceive me, that his cigarettes and his smoke doesn't fool everyone the way he wishes it to and that there's someone that sees right through him too, someone that knows he would appreciate a soft rose every single morning or a mug of coffee with heaps of sugar

i wish someone would tell him there's a good half of me that exists for him

a good half that sees into the smoke and hums his tunes before going to bed, tunes he think no one listens to.

because i do.

i fell for a boy i wasn't supposed to fall for, smiling a smile i'm not allowed to smile,

it's about this boy that lives down the street. he's not well off and lives without his parents. my dad asks me to stay away from him, his ash tray and second hand guitar a bit too intimidating,

my dad thinks your clothes are dirty and that you don't know how to talk to elders, or carry yourself, or have morals like we're all accustomed to,

and i,

i wonder what the colour of your room is.

we were naked and he made a cocoon of blankets around us, white plain silk sheets.

"i could make you feel the fireworks, you know?

and sniff the magic,

or hear the glitter."

he murmured in the quiet of whiteness. small chirps and swirls of cheese being bitten coming from the rat holes. i hummed to him, thinking,

"you already do,"

i murmur with my first two fingers interlocked with his first two fringes. he looks at me from where his head is laid on my waist, smiling. i lift my head, going forward and sniff the black and brown on his cheekbones.

now i know what his beard smells like.

its black and different shades of brown. his eyelashes dance the phenomenon of parallelism when he nudges his nose into my navel and i laugh. and i just don't laugh. i laugh the way i'm not allowed to laugh, with my tongue out and snorts coming out every few seconds.

he lights a smoke and i take a drag. it hurts my throat but it reminds me so much of him that not smoking feels like incompletion and thats too painful, and because this person is a human kill. his eyes a kill and his beard a kill and his smile a kill and his music a kill.

his fingertips have raw brown scars but he still strings the chords on the guitar, cigarette dangling from his lips and his eyes a honey brown shining off the metal of the corning of the bed.

he sings a song about making a home in what you're taught as a hell, making a home outside of where you're supposed to comfortably belong, live, and die, about breaking your roots, stopping the breeding in your own field, jumping to a field you're scared of, inter coursing, and giving birth to the most beautiful form of species possible, a flower that can't be bought with money or even with home love. unreachable. inevitable. priceless.

just like the boy i wasn't allowed to fall in love with, but did.

There's So Much Pain

there's a lot of pain in this world.

there are mothers with broken hearts. lovers with broken souls. fathers with uneven heartbeats. there are kids who don't belong and teens that don't know what home is

there's so much, so much sadness

and that's why i say its a wonder. its a wonder we still exist.

because pain is a beauty but beauties come with a cost, always. you pay your price, make your sacrifice — be in pain

but i ask you

love,

do not suffer

for there is already a lot of pain in this world

there are killers with broken legs and soldiers who don't return home

so do the wonders you can, and smile every once in a while

for you bear the beauty of pain

so let the beauty award you the happiness

the smile, the shimmer, the glitter

and don't be what you've been for your happiness, a killer

give birth to curves for your lips and air for your mouth

so do wonders you can, and smile

smile every once in a while

because its a wonder we still exist

for there is already a lot of pain in this world

humans that can't see

or souls that can't speak

people that can't dance for moving is their life and kids that might never know what a melody is

so don't be what you've been for your happiness, a knife

give birth to life for your eyes and existence for the blue in them

do wonders you can, and smile

smile every once for a while

sketch4.jpg

Red Wine

i had red wine today

we loved kissing but it was always me kissing. we made love but it was almost always just like fucking. i wish i could tell you i hated it that you got in my favourite drink after we did all that. i wish i could tell you that i love red wine and you make me hate it.

i wanted red wine during fucking and making love but sometimes - sometimes i wouldn't mind a nice dinner. no fancy candles but a matchstick would do too. i'm not asking for big meals but your company would be just fine.

i think i didn't ask for the big things and that's why you fell in love with me thinking i wouldn't want the small things either.

That's false

all loves need the small things, the candles and conversations, the being and the existing, the breathing and the dying sleeps.

i wanted red wine during fucking and making love but sometimes, sometimes i wouldn't mind a nice talk too, about days, aspirations, dreams, goals and confessions. confessions about what we hate about each other, talks about making things better. talks about where this goes. talks about having red wine in meaningful moments because its what calms me and you made me fucking hate it.

and its been four years

i didn't find anyone else after you

i had red wine today and it made me think of you

and

and its been four years

but in all loyalty,

sitting here in this street side restaurant with a broken ceiling and noisy chairs, having red wine in plastic cups with cubes of ice all by myself made me realise

that sometimes you need to lose others in order to find yourself

and i wouldn't change this treasure for the world.

Lonely Is Lovely

he thinks

sometimes i think lonely is beautiful

lonely in a tent away from the world with someone

celebrating nudity with chocolate chip ice creams and frozen sundaes and popcorns and movies

surrounded with aura of smelly home cooked food

the blankets are a bold brown and if you look closely you find darker brown spots, the much bolder spots

"i think sometimes if life's cycle was this. birth, ten days in a lonely tent with your lonely someone, and then death," she whispered so low that her voice had a natural melodious whistle that shrilled all the hair on my skin

"live, make love, and die," she looked at me,

i could spot three pieces of popcorn in her hair and i wanted to eat those. there was a bit smudged butter on her hairline and i wanted to lick that, and i wondered about a life like that, a life with only longing of love and no search, only life, love, and death. living with love and dying with love.

with indents of your lovers' lips raw on the inside of your thigh.

imagine dying like that

dying with raw indents of love

i closed my eyes with her face fading into a shiny black image behind my eyelids and lashes and rhymed our breaths together, inhale and exhale together, slowly rising and slowly falling. and i think yes.

yes lonely is beautiful. lonely in a tent away from the world with someone

lonely with my glitter. yeah she's glitter. so much spread glitter. shimmering and bright, you think it'll hurt your eyes but the shine bounces off your iris and forms a linear pattern on your face and its the kind of shine you can't gather. its touchable but uncontrollable.

she thinks

we just bask in nature like Adam and Eve

at least we can pretend to be

we can pretend there's no bad air and trash

or politics and media

there's nothing like a gay or lesbian or nothing like a rich or poor

there's just

just touch, the human touch

the magical touch by soft pads of a fingertip of your lover

the lines and small linear moons on the thumb you reckon you could fill with your glitter

damp lips that bite into the thread of the blanket or the plump of a lip or secretive smiles exchanged with the back of my head

i catch it all but he doesn't know

he's too lost in the nature of the glitter we create together like fairy lights hung from the ceiling of a mansion

but its nothing like a mansion and its just a tent and the two of us

and idea of life of a twenty four into ten and death

and death to me, darling, has never seemed oh so lovely

Them

humans don't know

    but we decorate our death with the glitter

    together

    we path out the maps we want to travel and the foods we wish to eat

    lost in nature like Adam and Eve

    together

    we bask in nature the festival of love making

    together

    like Adam

    like Eve

I Couldn't Draw Her

i just couldn't get myself to do it.

i couldn't draw her.

cause no amount of perfectly transcended brushes or shades or paints would do justice to that gold of a heart. the way she lights up when she talks about her passion and the way her eyes do that sad-happy thing when she's drunk and blurting out all her dirty old skeletons. i just can't bring myself to plaster a copy of her being and soul, how enormously beautiful she is while she eats or sleeps or writes or just is.

it's like you create something beautiful in that extremely lucky moment of yours, and then its gone - and then you just cannot create anything like that ever again. like artists block. because its just too good to be made twice, or have a second version to it.

yeah

she's like that,

like created in that enormously blessed random moment, unknowingly, unintentionally, and then the moment was gone and so no one will be as perfect as her, as bluntly beautiful as her. no art like that could be ever made again.

and she's all that

she's not smoking up and vodka

she's art, and creativity

and i dream that she's drunk but she's still holding onto my hand like its her little globe and my fingertips the tiny little stars

tracing the back of my wrist like writing stories on my skin is her favourite hobby attaching her hip to mine in a soft click

her being is a work of art and her existence, a pleasurable process full of creativity

she's all black and at the same time some colours i've never seen before

and she's all that

she's art, and creativity

and i can't do anything because she's not mine to be. she's not mine to draw. but i still cheat in a line or two, the way her shoulders bow done when she walks past me across the hall and the way her clothes are almost always hanging loosely across her timid frame. she holds her sketchbooks like her lifelines and i'm always curious to peek in a look or two

and she thrills this protective urge in me. she stumbles a bit and i want to reach out to her and hold her and let her know that as long as i'm around there's nothing that could humanly hurt her

she's soft and harsh, short and long strokes of brushes against the canvas, she's like knives dipped deeply into honey to paint enticing witchcraft, masking her vivid appearance in more magical elements like red lukewarm paint that might even taste good if you dip the tip of your tongue into it.

she's all the conversations over coffee you crave on your bad days with people who want to go beyond just the beautified border of your heart

and hugs you die to get, like holding so close, trying to heal the other person in that embrace of yours with your lips near their ears whispering encouragement to never give up,

yeah, she's a hug like that

yeah, she'll all that

and much, much more.

We Love Train Rides

we loved train rides

    couches face front with a small brown table in between, smell of rusty metal and brushed corners of the doors

    they slide rough against the ceiling and floor, alarming arrivals and departures of persons

    special person

    kind old people came every few hours selling snacks and candies to our aged tongues

    i remember our tongues when we were young

    slurping the taste of lolly and swoops of ice cream

    and kissing

    kissing a lot

    in the same booth, on the same couch, in the same train, in the same daze

    19 or 99

    the tongues are the same pink

    with germs and stuck foods

a little bit of saliva of your loved one and a homey taste of your own

19 or 99

the kisses became slow

but never stopped

the kisses became sloppier

but never stopped

the kisses became firmer

and they never stopped

we made eye contact under the pool back home basking the sting of chlorine

sometimes blowing air onto the window, drawing hearts and patterns

celebrating concepts of forever

we love train rides

couches face front with a small brown table in between, smell of rusty old metal and brushed corners of the doors

different seasons face the window of the cabin

daze of the nights and knights of the days

the charm, the beauty, the nature's game

19 or 99

it all stays the same

we share bits of blueberry muffin back and forth and i look at him *he's aged but the his bow is the same red, the suspenders stretch the same and the round of his belly is the same. i see a few hair on his chest and the world of a pattern that his eyebrows make when furrowed. he takes vanilla always - ice cream, and scented candles in our home. his favourite colour is vanilla too. but his bow stays the same red. i like red. everyone thinks his eyes are blue i've always thought the right one to be a darker green. i think his eyelashes fan my face better than anything else and his eyeballs do this magical thing which ain't human. my lionhearted lover. his nails have turned dark brown in the borders and they curve in like his body is trying to save itself.*

i know some day he will decay.

and so will i

but oh

we still kiss so slow, so firm, so soft. we still eat all the bits of blueberry, and drops of vanilla. his adams apple still bobs when i come too close or when i stare too long. he's aged but his bow is the same red, we're 99 but there's nothing about us that says dead. he's still roses on Sundays and kisses before work and bed, he still the same 9 in 19 or 99.

my lionhearted lover.

Days Like That

it's hard on some days. it's hard getting out of the bed and rushing off to do something you actually love more than life itself but not having that energy in you, not knowing why. not feeling confident enough to lift up your eyes and look at yourself, or hearing but at the same time not listening what the other people are saying. failing to process a single word. as though you're trapped in a small invisible circle around you. the one that alternatively seems like a protective shield. but is actually a trap.

    on days like that - you stay home. you stay home and hone yourself. your inner self. look at yourself in the mirror and ask your face to relax. don't ask your lips to smile, but simply leave them hanging. let your hair be. dip your fingers in a pool of paint and play with it. listen to a piece of music that reminds you of your best memory, and then revisit that time in your mind. grab a warm cup of hot chocolate, and just hold the cup as if it's your friend. inhale the warm protective smell. probably let out a few tears, and just keep holding the cup as long as it's warmth has traveled to the farthest point within your body. warming you up internally. go through old photographs, the ones that carry that rusty old smell with them, the ones that are from the moments you probably don't even know existed. look out and try to stare at nothing, letting your eyes go blank. take a black pen and draw on your own hand - a flower, a simple word, your own name, anything. lie down on the hard floor and just look up at the ceiling, the lights in your room, the window, and inhale the scent of your own home.

don't let your body and mind fall into the happenings of that day, instead, make things happen for yourself. days like these are meant for realisation of the fact that life is beautiful in small bits. some days you just have to give up on the outside world and just be with yourself. Give yourself some time for you. smile because of your own self. There's simply nothing more beautiful in this world than being at peace with your own company

Not Apologising

i worked out for 2 hours where as i'd thought i'd work out for 4. i guess i've miserably failed the diet i was trying to follow. i asked a question that was laughed at. i looked at myself in the mirror and wished to look away instantly. my assignment didn't turn out as good as i had expected it to. and i hurt someone i shouldn't have.

i think i am not at my best today. but then again, am i supposed to be at my best every day of my life? isn't that what we're told?

but i guess we mistake 'giving our best every day' with 'being the best everyday'. you don't have to be at your best all the damn time. it's okay for wanting to do average and just have one of those normal days. it's okay for not wanting to fight out there every day to prove yourself. there are things you want to excel at and there are things you like being average at, and that's what makes you special.

and no, don't ask for forgiveness. don't apologise cause you think you couldn't do your best during the day. you want to fail a little and get back up again to fight, that's what you want. that's what makes you blossom, not the constant perfection.

you blossom every day - *a little.*

A Letter for Your Loss

i try to look up around me, but even amidst the darkness of midnight the surroundings seem to hurt my eyes. i can't look up. it aches. i don't have beautiful hands but i'd rather look at them.

knitting my brows together. playing with the rubber band on my hand. tugging back a few strands of my hair. chewing on a small part of my t-shirt. my smudged mascara irritating my eye. vision slightly blurred. anything that touches my skin - a leaf, a piece of paper, a human hand, wind. it's scary. touches are scary. delicate touches are even more painful.

i heard hugs hold a strong therapeutic power, do they? i haven't been *really* hugged in a while, since she left last month. so sometimes i go and sit in this bathroom cubicle of my college and wrap my arms around myself. it doesn't really make a difference though.

"i just can't find the right words to say to you - to myself. i just want to say that..that, *that it's okay if you're not okay*. and i will be here with you to share that. i'm not going anywhere."

he wrapped his arms around me. i look at the direction of the voice - the slouched depressed shoulders, rough stubble, hollow and the lacklustre eyes on his face not allowing to recognise the man beside me. he looks like beat. his hugs aren't as warm as they used to be.

he smells of cigarettes, mint, misery, and faltered fatherhood. he reminds me of a black canvas - stubborn enough to not let any colours show, even if it's just blunt white misery.

it is almost like she took dad with her as well. he doesn't talk to me anymore. of course he blurts words and sentences to me - but he doesn't really *talk* to me. he just stares at things, random things, and sometimes not even that. i don't complain, or demand. not because i guess i understand, but because i guess i've lost the energy to process.

i rest the bunch of flowers on sand. pure wet sand. layers below lays a body whose hugs i loved the most. it was what i needed to make a good day a better day and a better day the best day. i missed her. ironically, there's something good about this place that sticks to my mind like a good song, communicating that this place is safe, that it's almost okay for wanting to come here every day and unfold all the stiff edges of my aching soul.

i couldn't look at people anymore because their sympathetic eyes allowed me to cry just more and more and indulge in self-pity. but the beautiful lady down in the grave had taught me better. i knew i was miserable and i knew that was okay. i knew that for the 17 years that she was here, she had taught me so much - she taught me to entangle myself, to forgive and to start afresh, to not give up at times like these.

oh, she taught me so much.

abandoning my school bag on the ground, i engulfed the mixed scent of wet sand and flowers. the evening smells like old rain, ozone and metal. fallen leaves swirling in the wind and tugging sarcastically at my stiff figure, nudging me to *just let go.*

i could smell *her* too. i could sense her touching me through the strong wind blowing. even if i couldn't sense it on my own skin, i could feel it within me. she was engulfing me in a hug. i shut my eyes tight as the overwhelming feeling of revisiting home sprinkles itself upon me. i wasn't crying no more. i could feel a very familiar pair of hands wrap around me. i smiled faintly. o*nly* a mother - or, her memory, could make you smile at times like these.

i had not been *really* hugged since she had left,

and *she knew*.

a letter for your loss

Reading Love

and these days i just tend to sleep in. i don't wish to do the things i once wanted to. i love them, i love it all, i really do, but i just can't get my body to move or make an effort. no, i'm not lazy. i'm a hard worker and it is something i take pride in.

but somedays i can't help but feel this numbness settle in, and i can't register people's words, the sentences their mouths form, their expressions and their laughs and their jokes and their logics. it stops making sense. i feel like i'm stepping into fire the moment i unlock my brown front door and tend to walk out and face things. the faded pink leaves and the sweet scented summer wind stops appealing to me. and i close the door again.

the idea of eating makes me sick at the outset and caffeine is all i think about. it soothes my body in an ascending warmth traveling from my throat to my wiggling toes. its almost as if someone just put a protective shield over me.

and i read.

i read to forget and to be forgotten — to elate new wounds and to heal the aged ones.

i read to escape, to decamp, to bolt.

printed letters that temporarily dissolve the aching lump at the back of my throat, and — i cry. i hold the book and i cry. i mentally talk myself into something warm embosoming me. its not a person and its not a thing. i don't even know what it is — i just know that it exists and that its keeping me warm when i'm immobilised and cold. and it benumbs me to my pain, to the weird things i feel. ones, i refuse to give a rationale for.

a blanket with a foul odour is wrapped around my shoulders so yeah it's pretty warm, contrasting to my cold freezing skin. It's not that ice freezing cold, it's just that deadened and desensitised kind of cold.

this is life happening, isn't it?

Unlike

don't be afraid. break a heart if you have to, break it because yours isn't in it anymore, and the other would be better off without you, they deserve better. you won't be judged. skip an exam if you have to, skip it because it's okay to take it easy once in a while, it's okay to give a re-exam. it does not make you a bad student. break a rule, break it because you deserve that thrill, and because somewhere around you want to. you won't be sentenced to termination of happiness.

read a book you hate

watch a movie you despise

forgive a person who didn't ask for forgiveness

take an off from the gym if you have to

have 3 slices of pizza instead of 1

kiss him first

make the first move

wear something you're not comfortable in

visit a place which is sphinx-like

try boxing because you detest it

hold on tighter if you have to

and let go if you need to

lick your fingers the way you like it

go braless

snort when it's not appropriate

smile when not needed —

let the tears fall

do things you reckon you wouldn't if you were in your senses.

because i'm here to tell you that no matter what, you're a good person.

Best Friends With an Introvert

and when on your bad kinda days you snap, and you're tired of all the perfect smiles and the perfect outings and the perfection of people around you, and the countless lies about love, friendship, society, studies, that are shoved up your ass - you'll go to this friend. and she'll give you her most favourite jumper, one that's lose and hangs off your shoulder but is purely warm. she'll let you have the best side of the couch, because it sinks in just perfect and right and makes you feel protected, and she wants you to feel like that because she knows you need it.

she'll make the best hot chocolate for you and add 5 sips of vodka in it because she knows you need that too. 5 precisely because you need to loosen up but at the same time be yourself. she knows your verge. she'll sit on the other end and let you keep your legs on her laps. and she'll talk.

she won't tell you about how amazing you are, but she'll tell you that you're blessed and that if you're going through a bad phase, its probably life happening to you. she won't tell you you're pretty or beautiful, but she'll tell you that you are you and not everybody can be that, not everyone can snort on sucky jokes the way that you do and not everyone can comfort a person the way you do. she won't tell you to not to be miserable, but she'll rather tell you to be friends with that misery, because she knows thats what's gonna make you grow the most. and she'll make you enjoy this misery, this sadness of your life.

and at the end she's gonna randomly smile at you and switch on the TV and let you be. and after a while she'll tell you about this really small cafe down town, one that sells ridiculously cheap and yummy coffee, promising you to take you there, as if nothing's wrong.

and then you realise, nothing really is. It's all okay. and you count on her promise, because you know her promises are real, and they mean something to you and to her.

and then you'll think how dependent you are on this person, who makes you feel that its okay to not be okay, who doesn't call you an attention seeker when you actually talk about not being okay, who doesn't complain when you're not there to listen to her issues and problems because you have this party to go to, and she lets it go, she doesn't complain about you not being there, because she probably doesn't need you as much as you need her. she is actually pretty much okay on her own. and that thought scares you somewhere around.

but you still smile, because you know this person, you know this person who sniffs and hugs books on a bad day, who rankles her heart out on a piece of paper and makes the best hot chocolate in the whole damn world. she is not there in every great moment of your life, because she is behind them.

she kept you going.

she'll keep you going without you even knowing.

The Thing That Saved You

"you did it," the figure in front of me kept her warm hand over my knotted nervous fingers. i couldn't help but look at her.

"you really did it. in the beginning of the sessions you had said that life isn't for you. and look at you *today, right now, at this moment.* you really made it!"

i smiled at her and walked out of the room, clutching *it* closely to my chest. my dad smiled down at me and walked towards the car. i put on my seatbelt and involuntarily smiled to myself looking down at *it*, my therapist's words sinking in.

it's not like i didn't reach out for help. i did try to talk to people about it, but i realised that they just don't get it. sometimes the pain or that uneasy feeling in my chest - i cannot explain it in words, and that makes me feel that maybe words to describe that kind of a murderous feeling just don't exist.

and then i just stopped. i stopped explaining, i stopped trying, i surrendered, i stopped trying to live, i came at peace with the dullness. inside myself. i let it engulf me in the best possible manner. not leaving an inch on my skin that would allow me to maybe escape back. i thought about my broken dreams, about all the spirits that ditched me.

although somewhere around my heart is telling me that its not my fault, that heartbreaks and failures are a part of growing up.

that until and unless my fingers don't encounter that sting of pain from the thorns of the rose stem - my skin won't learn to appreciate the softness of the petals and the life that it gave me.

but then i'm smiling now, my lips curling up without me even intending them to.

i look down at the 'it' that saved me - a book my therapist randomly suggested for entertainment. it was a love story. and the moment she had mentioned it, i had laughed at her. i'd laughed at her.

but i gave it a read. i read it anyway. i didn't think about it making my life better.

i didn't expect to fall in love with the characters and the abrupt ending of the book. i didn't expect that curious urge to grow in the strong pit of my stomach for wanting to visit that extremely small town in the outskirts of London, which consists of a population of less than 2,000 people, but had been described so beautifully by that random author - that i ended up planting my own idea of home in that town i hadn't even heard of a month ago.

i didn't intend to, but i fell in love with the way the author's words gave me hope, gave my life hope, it gave me a reason to get out of my bed every day, take a walk and sit on the bench with a warm cup of coffee and start reading again.

i just fell in love with the oddest of things.

i fell in love with the way the author described the lives of the two completely opposite individuals, the way the girl in the book wore button ups and people made fun of it, called her manly, but she wore it anyway because she loved it. i fell in love with the way the author described the beauty of a small town which is a small family in itself, the way their first date consisted of exchanging different CD's for kisses, the way that there was only one pub in the whole damn town. i fell in love with the way they both went to that old rusty pub with the same stale glass bar, that old pool table, a small tv at the right most corner, every weekend of every month, back to back for forty eight years.

i fell in love with the way the guy coming from London fell in love with the small town and just decided to live there for the rest of his life, and the way he created *a house and a home* for her, amidst a small town which consists of just one pub, amidst a place where they never wanted *more*, amidst a happy place that i'd thought didn't exist.

— and i fell in love with the way the book made me realise that you don't find a happy place, but you make a place your happy place.

the book is not a bestseller, but it saved me. and i realise that everyone's got something of that sort. something that saves them when they need to be saved. it can be an old senseless movie, a random bunch of words said by someone, a gesture, a song, a painting, an old toy, a superhero miniature you got when you were 5, a torn piece of cloth from your mom's warmest jumper - anything.

and that this random book written by this random author which is not a bestseller actually saved my fucking life. and its *my book*.

the book came along when i needed saving. it just came along.

its just that uncommon feeling you develop for an object, for a song, a movie, or maybe just a movie scene, a toy. you have a problem, and you go to this thing. you watch that movie again, you read that book again, you look at that painting again, you caress that old toy again. you revisit it, and it gives you strength. it gives you hope. it doesn't make sense, really, and that's the best part about it.

sometimes people are saved by other people, and sometimes people are saved by art - and i couldn't be more thankful for belonging to the latter.

I'd Be the Same Happy

i couldn't find happiness.

i tried but i couldn't. and this is the most lost i've ever felt in the last 16 years of my being.

so instead I moved to other things - inanimate objects, that actually happened to have more promising life than living beings.

i found happiness in flowers

even the rotten ones for the way they lived as long as they could. i found happiness in the green grass, the one filled with mud as well because of the way it stayed grounded no matter what.

i found happiness in books, not only by reading them but by holding them whenever i felt weak or felt like i don't belong here. i found happiness in words and poems by anonymous people, for they comforted a stranger like me without disclosing their identity for appreciation.

i found happiness in blank papers, for they gave me wings and independence of doing whatever

i wanted to do, draw whatever i wish to draw and write whatever i wish to write.

i found happiness in unpredictable weather changes and unsolicited rain by other people, for it made me walk in the cold weather without a jacket, shivering and trembling, and ultimately gave me the comfort of having the warmest cup of the tea on my couch later in the day.

i found happiness in watching people walk,

random people with random thoughts and random directions,

the ones tripping over and spilling coffee all over their office clothes and the ones leaning on the pole of the street to steal an unforeseen kiss,

i found happiness in different expressions of love, the way her dad won't let go of her finger or the way her mum would let her have the last bite of the cake despite her hunger, or the intrigued way i sometimes see people sitting beside each other just for the sake of it, when they don't have anything to talk about but they'd just rather sit with each other than away from each other.

i found happiness in the warmth of my winter coat as i walked back home alone, and the mood decided to flay the happiest kind of light over the streets and the side walks. i found happiness in my lived apartment, dirty corners and the foul odour from the kitchen skin. i found happiness in the familiar scent of my existence in my home.

you give me your precious worn out winter jumper or you give me a diamond ring, i'd be the same happy

you make me a warm cup of coffee or buy me a fancy dinner, i'd be the same happy you take me across the country for a vacation or you show me your favourite secret alley, i'd be the same happy

you tell me how your day was like you've waited the entire day just to talk to me or you say nothing but sit beside me to share a time of silence,

i'd be the same happy.

Living the Lie

shut the door and whisper untrue things to me, tug me in the blanket and lie to me about your love, switch the bedside lamp off and make a tangled mess of our limbs. put your favourite music on and keep the window open, let the cold air blow in and dance in contrast with the warmth of your body against mine. let me live the lie peacefully, for a moment.

Love Ruins Love

i think

i think i'd rather look at things fall apart than give up and live a lie till my last exhale.

we are real. we are as real as the magicians magic is. we are real as long as you let us be. its alright if the kisses didn't feel the same after all these years, or the sex got a little dull. maybe we needed to work on things. maybe that's all there was. a little work. because isn't life all about that? a little effort? a little nudge and a push?

isn't life all about arms hovering behind to catch if you fall?

but every candle faces a dull death and i want to tell you that it was not okay to give up on us.

maybe watching things fall apart would've given us the strength to put the pieces back together and there are other candles to light the dull death. i still see the way you look at me, with atoms and every point of your skin, your goosebumps tickled pink to form a pattern of my name on your skin and,

my love, *my presence puts you on fire.*

i see the hidden gasps and hear the words your hearts' telling mine.

"this very night i wish for a long time. i don't know forever or a week, a month or a year, ten years or until we've alive. i want to wish for what i know, because there will come a day i'll grow old and my heart will pale on its own and there won't be any love and i don't want you around then. i don't want you around to see the ugly lines and marks of ageing, .the creases that warn death.

because love ruins love,

we're real. lets make love together,

and leave for good."

and i want to tell you ageing together is what realness is about, and that creases on your face are lines that let me look into your souls on days you shut yourself, because it says *I've known you a while* and i'm aware if your heart's not beating the same. my palms are a part of me and the warm bottle your heart needs when paleness arrives. but you've dislodged my arms before their arrival and i want to think maybe realness for two people can never be the same and it could be love but at the same time, it could be the real love or the love swimming in the pool of human practicality. the latter pains my very existence and i'm okay,

i'm okay if i have nowhere to go after this.

so here i'm stood watching the things fall apart all alone. the kitchen getting emptier and vanishing of the collection of refrigerator magnets from venice and paris. there's no bike keys and dirty muddy boots near the front door and cancellation of the magazine that arrives every week for you.

i'm sorry for your heart — for it was broken and denied the unconditional love awaiting right in front of it. and isn't that the hardest thing?

letting the love, ruin our love?

Photograph

why do you keep them then? she asks.

we're alive, he said, we're alive because of them.

tucked away in the ancient closeted silver box

the roll of your camera

the albums lined in the cupboard

and shelf of your room.

the smiles you think of

the laughs that echo off your ears

the ghostly sensation of the touches you gasp at

the polaroids stuck on the walls mean a life well lived. its because the photographs you have that are blurred and perfect at the same time. they actually caught the laugh, the kiss, the pain in the moment in that dim eye, the tear stain on the camera lens, the misty hand shake, the hazy smile.

the photographs

they are an ecstasy

it was a foggy night, i see the wet stain of the snow in the corner of the photograph, i see my loved ones walking hand in hand with drops of water falling off the slope of the houses beside them, they hold an umbrella, its dark blue and it feels so real. i wish i had an umbrella. i press the fingers holding the photograph in between because suddenly,

suddenly i'm very cold.

in the photograph, there's a smile etched on my face but i know it, i know the photograph captured doesn't lie and there are unshed tears in my eyes, and i wish, i wish he sees this photo because he needs to see the dismissal of love.

the next photograph is a lip lock. i close my eyes when i hold it and suddenly he's catching my breath with an open mouth, and osculation of his front against my back. its the touch of my love, this moment, this kiss. my whole body shakes as the photograph slips from my fingertips and i think it hurts a little. the slip hurts a little and the moment hurts a bit more. the shine of the sun aches my eyes and,

and i might not keep the image. but i'll keep the photograph, i'll keep the moment - i'll keep the love.

thousands catch the vision, but how many catch the moment?

You're you

in the mirror you see yourself the way you want to see yourself

and pictures are taken by people the way they see you

so really

what's the real you, beneath all dirt and grim?

i'll tell you

you are you when you're not watched

you are you while you drop 2 drops of soup and moan out loud at twelve am

you are you with clothes that don't belong to you and with your used make up wipe around the room

you are you when you swim naked in the lake and there on the side, beside you, watching you, sits a man who's writing poems about you

and when you stare at the fountains with wonder or sit by the lake trying your hand at writing, missing home that's miles away, thinking about calling people and saying things

saying that you love solitude but not loneliness and, and you're lonely you're lonely as you're here trying to write what your heart instructs you to yet its the wounded blood in your veins that dances your fingers

you're you when you're tempted to self harm because that's you too

but there's a piece of every bone and muscle in you that's dead, and you killed it.

its you, this is you sometimes too.

but you're flowers as well, love

you're flowers in a desert and waves of love in a war

you're peace when there's anxiety and the call of hope when the heartbeat of your loved one stops

you're so much to everyone around you just by being you

so don't let the cameras and the mirrors fool you.

you're deep kisses on cellulite and love bites on brown scars

you're the skimming of lips on uneven skin and nuzzling in unrevealed corners of the body

you're like the things some people might never discover in their whole existence

Life

there's life

    in the way

    you just breathe

Wish

how many nights do you wish you could say that you wanted to stay and that it doesn't matter if you've got places to go or things to do because this matters more

    how many nights

    do you wish you had

    fucked firmer

    kissed harder

    held tighter

    called a little

    a little more closer

Dead Petals & I

dead petals and i

    kissing each petal

    i murmured

    "don't forget to breathe,"

    sometimes

    sometimes we forget to exist

Self Love

we don't realise it but the roots of our self love are so deeply rooted in the ones we sin to love.

How's Love Beautiful?

sometimes i think how's love beautiful

    when i bleed words and veins onto papers

    praying to a someone for a someone

    a someone who made love a choice

    how's love beautiful like this

    when there's a thin thread and two people hanging so low and deep

    with boiling iron and lava beneath

    how's love beautiful like this

    when you think of a broken heart and how there'll always be that lost piece of puzzle abandoned and forgotten in the corner,

    that for granted declaration of love

    that unanswered pray

    and that desperate plea of fixture

    how's love beautiful like this?

    he looks me in the eye and walks away

and what hurt the most

is he looked me in the eye like he *knew*

my lower lip trembling, i whisper, *"i'll always be praying, for my unanswered pray."*

I Can Read You

i don't know how to speak

or hear

but i can read

i can read the language of water dribbles sliding down your skin

i can read the vocals of open mouthed gasps in the air

i can read you

You Saved Me

you don't know

    we met at the edge of the bridge

    my feet hanging off the rail

    your eyes on my iced nose and ears

    you looked like you saw past the shaded pink of my cheeks and nose and saw the paleness

    like you saw the reasons

    and that for a moment you'd say its justified

    its justified for you to jump

    "but darling, its only justified if you want it to be. the stars will shine only if you look at them and the sun will rise only if you open the curtains. you can jump, i won't judge you. but i, i do not speak for the stars and the sun that kept you alive. i do not speak for your atoms and their wish to be alive, their plea for another chance, the begging of your pale face for another go. because maybe giving up is justified sometimes but jumping off a bridge isn't,"

    you don't know me

    but you saved me jumping off a bridge

    sketch5.jpg ¬

Our Little Noses

i felt so weak when your nose kissed mine.

it was in the middle of the cold winter of 2016 and it felt like a new year already

i felt the freckles of your skin pinprick against mine

knocking the air out of the trees in my lungs

the flowers in my throats

the roots in my stomach

i lift my fingers - befriending the whistling of my tongue and your gaze

i feel the surface of your nose

i feel your softness against the roughness of my skin

the freckles forming an elegant motif of our existence *together*

the contact of our noses puts words in my mouth like i love you but i don't say it because the motif we created together does and there's nothing like it

there's nothing like my weakness and your nose kissing mine in the middle of the cold winter of 2016 and i know,

i know 2017 has been a great year already.

You're Black

you're really black i think, the way you breathe in the smoke, the cloud of mist around your lips and the texture of your skin. you're black in ways you look, the presence osculating from your being and shine beaming off your feet, you're black in the way you exist, with eyes silhouetted like diamonds and sensations of the words you speak.

you're black in the way you think, without any boundaries, without a yes or a no, with a wrong or a right, you're the black surrounding the moon and the stars.

Some Hearts Don't Heal

cigarettes.

they are harmful

she knows - its an open invitation for more dependency on something. and dependency is brutally painful.

screeching the weirdest of points and lines and areas on your body and its painful

but she allows herself this moment, early in the morning, where people are yet to come out of their houses and all the pale green and yellow leaves with drops of cool water are untouched. a decayed shade of dark orange is peeking out of the peripheral end of the sky, from all the way down to the end of the road,

its harmful, dangerous, unhealthy? and of course,

'it kills'

but she allows herself this one bad habit,

even going harshly against the pleading call of her lungs that it doesn't soothe her the way a cigarette is actually supposed to soothe a smoker.

but it kinda does settle her — ground her — in a different way.

she misses someone

they — they just — *they just simply smell like him*

like nuzzling her nose to his shoulder in the quiet winter of 2006

or kissing the tip of his fingertips and inhaling the dark smell of cigarettes mediating from his body on a Sunday night with pizza boxes launched randomly around the room

the ill-lit grey clouds puff out of her nose and mouth, and a weird irritation takes birth at the back of her throat. it doesn't suit her. she's someone who'd rather go for a jog to level out her stress rather than smoke.

but the cigarettes — the smell — the smoke — the dizziness — *its all him.*

and it fucking breaks her heart that shrinks and becomes 100 times more smaller on mornings like these because she misses him so much even after all these years. her heart's not broken, but has actually been breaking more and more with every passing day, this daunting realisation settling in.

there are hearts that are broken, the ones that carry this crack that is over time maybe healed if you're lucky, or at least fixed with other blessings in your life.

a bright yellow ray peaks across her heavy lidded lashes and she looks up to see the sun has risen. she looks across the neighbourhood and sees that old lady come out of her house, collecting milk from the corner of the door.

the lady looks up and passes her a smile, a smile that says she knows, a small nod and a tiny sigh conveying nothing but just the fact that *'life really doesn't stop.'*

and even though the sun has arrived with all the lights and brightness and birds chirping and people unnerving,

the lane coming to life,

all she sees is darkness, a dullness,

an irreplaceable dark black shade over the layer of her eyes and her soul,

even amidst a luminosity that's as lively as a healthy new born baby.

how do you heal this kind of a pain?

its surprisingly comfortable — because it makes her feel that — that she's *not out there* - she's not fighting or taking up challenges, she's just living the mediocrity, that she's in a confined place prisoned by his beautiful homicidal memories and it's actually alright — *its home, because its him.*

the dullness and the darkness help her get through it,

through her job

through work

and through the expectations of fellow humans

through this for granted love lying heavy in her chest

being ignored in undeniable pain.

a pain hurts a little more every day.

but she knows.

she'd rather live with pain that belongs to him, than not living with the traces of his fragmented existence at all

its home, because its him

the nicotine biologically travels to her lungs and emotionally to her heart. the grey faded smoke flattering across the cracks and, *fuck —*

its sudden sensations at night

tranquilising cold saliva tracing her waist

intimate presses on inner thighs

soft subdued knuckles nudging to put her to sleep — soothing right across her raw and aged wounds.

its a healing caress that only lasts for a couple of holy seconds before the smoke is fleeing out of her mouth, only to let the ache return.

and sometimes it's like the blood that runs in her veins is trying to assassinate her. the smoke — *his smell* — she closes her eyes in exhaustion and her lower lip trembles painfully

she internally scoffs at the lack of tears in her eyes.

there comes a point in life, a point in the circle of pain that goes beyond tears, and thats even worse, this point is full of hollowness and blankness, dry cheeks and numb eyelids, chapped lips and trembling hands - and you wish you could cry, you wish you had tears to cry and build an outlet.

she feels a blazing sensation on her fingertips and realises that her cigarettes' burnt out. she takes another drag of his partial existence and throws it on the ground to stub it out.

she shakes her head to get over the feeling, she shakes her hands a bit and squints her eyes, feeling disgusting dryness settle in her mouth. she straightens her posture and smiles, she smiles to herself.

a rehearsal for the rest of the day.

she gets to work and resumes writing the ending chapter of her unfinished book based on belongingness, partially eyeing her jumpy agent from the corner of her eyes, looking at her in hope of yet another draft.

sighing, shutting off her mind, and letting her fingertips deal with it.

i was told about this normal conventional love - in school by my friends and in the middle of a curious hour at night by my mum with her tucked in with me in my comforter. about making love, and dates and flowers, car rides and fights, vacations and break ups, more sex and dinner dates, weak moments but good memories. it seemed - nice? something i looked forward to feeling, and having in life. but i never got to this type.

i, instead, got to this unconventional love - one that i hadn't been warned about.

i know this unconventional love that is a scientific pull — a destruction in the name and idea of therapy — an unfixable mistake — a skin deep craving — an addicting scar — a moan of pleasure mixed with a cry of pain — i've known love in his long calloused fingertips, uneven finger nails and a sweater with three holes, i've known love with eye talks and lose interlocked fingers, i've known love in random nibbling of my ear lobe and a tangled mess of limbs instead of a conventional hug, i've known love in stolen lunch bites and sneaked in wine bottles, love in a dark aisle and a ground full of wet mud, the unusual kisses of our bodies instead of just lips, and inhaling his exhaled air, i've known the love full of void moans and slap of skin against skin in a too quite room, i've known the love of messing up his tea every morning and burning his shirt, the love of falling down the bed while making love and kissing the dimples at his lower back, i've known the love of feeling too much of everything, not only happiness but sorrow - a kind of sorrow i've never felt before, the kind of cries i hadn't imaged would be possible to be cried, the kind of laughs that i thought only existed in movies and were too good to be true, a kind of warmth that pools in a permanent thirst in your soul - one you can't help but weep about.

it's the love in the name of belongingness - it's the love in the name of your being existing with him, of your self worth and your smiles and sorrows that have created a pathway going through his being. its dependent and its scary - its fucking scary. it's worse than an open heart surgery without anaesthesia or a growing untraceable cancer travelling in your body. it's worse than that moment of drowning where you feel you're going to die right before a pair of familiar hands drag you out.

but.

- but it's also flowers, it's your favourite childhood scent, and the faint warmth of your grand mom. it's also the tingles in your stomach and the drunkenness of your favorite warm red wine, it's the delight of your beloved returning from the dead and a lifelong dream coming true, it's a fixed wish you make by throwing a penny in the pond, it's an unpredictable smile at the end of a bad day and unexpected arms wrapped around your waist when you feel alone. it's swaying around the kitchen at 3 am in the night to a **sixties song** with boiling milk spilling out of the pot, it's your finger situated across his fingers while he plays the piano, it's a friend, a giving friend, a god sent friend.

it's an unbearable win.

i've known this unconventional love - this belongingness that goes way beyond just love, that goes way beyond passion and home. it's maddening. it's a belongingness that won't leave once settled in. one that's made me sniff a trace of the subject of my belongingness from the past 9 years.

i still find myself waking up at 4 am every morning, craving for nicotine and his partial presence.

and i know it doesn't go anywhere from this.

i tell myself every night before popping in the sleeping pill and placing a packet of marlboro on my bed side, under my warm but confining comforter, that tomorrow, i will not chase his memory - his source of partial existence in my life - i will not chase my belongingness - for my own betterment, i will let go.

and after every numb sixty minutes spent chain smoking every morning, in the end, its the same feeling, telling me that *you fool* - this painful belongingness that you're running away from is the fucking reason you're alive, or in no denial of the ache and need that's been there for his presence from the past 9 years — you would've died by now

the black whole? It grows every day.

it just grew an inch more.

i'm lonely, and i'm miserable.

but - i'm fine.

some hearts just don't heal.

And It's Like I'm Coming Home

time is a concept that fails to exist for me on all day, and i'm right here,

i don't remember rushing out of the office and getting in my car, i don't remember walking wildly towards the graveyard - as if it was my home. i sniffle back a tiny sob, my body radiates with uncomfortable head, and i try to remember that breathing is a thing.

i look at the hard stone and let out a laugh. it sounds sad to my own ears.

the grave stone reads - "a beloved brother, son, friend."

and i let out another sad laugh, looking around for absolutely nothing, with my teeth grazing my bottom lip. i smile, and the stretch across my cheeks feels sad too, and i think what a shame - what a shame it really is for the world around would never know how beautiful this person really was.

how he was beyond the bounds of just a brother, or a son, or a friend. how kind and caring, how irrevocably and annoyingly selfless he was.

is.

the stone.

that shouldn't be grey, because he was anything but. and because he's a colour that's yet to be discovered, a colour that carries so much effervescence and radiates so much positivity.

"hey you," i whisper,

and for the millionth time, i promise a faded promise to a faded someone, that i will start to live again. i will let myself heal. i will fall in love again. i will let go.

and as I'm whispering the faded promise to an uncertain someone, i bend down and touch the rough, hard stone, that is achingly smooth beneath my flat palm, and i feel a painful tug somewhere in my body that i can't put a finger upon.

and with each functioning cell and limb i faintly mutter, "i will never let go,"

and its like i'm coming home.

some hearts are just not meant to heal.

Shadow

i looked at her shadow. it had slumped shoulders. there was something her shadow said that she didn't. her shadow seemed oblivious to lies, to fear, to shame. but at the same time it seemed so, so familiar to pain.

her shadow had plump skin instead of plump lips, soft stretch marks and a bundled core like the strings of a guitar, only difference being she didn't know she was capable of so much music. her pubes were dark and i know light is what is preached but darling if at night everyone else is the dark background with you being the single star that travels across the planets with sweet burden of wishes of thousands of pleading hearts and souls. you're that star.

i looked at her shadow. it had slumped shoulders. i saw it all. i saw what she hid. i saw what she was asked to hide. i saw what it took to be called a plastic face. i saw the base on which plastic became a synonym for pretty.

fellow stars refuse to be your friends because you have a broken leg and you limp your way through the galaxy and darling you don't, but the world sees the trail of beautiful sparkle you leave behind with your limps followed by murmurs of hidden prayers and wishes to mend hearts of loved ones.

you hold a galaxy within you which you refuse to show because that galaxy is what fulfils the wishes of the thousand murmurs. so you keep the galaxy hidden for others' sake and let the other stars laugh their way through your limps.

i loosen my right shoulder, siding my face and sniffing the end of my collarbone, a thin layer of sweat shining and a drop or two bundled at the edge. i take a deep breath and remind myself its okay - its okay if on some day loving myself seems like the biggest task in the world and its okay if its so hard. hard is whats softening the rugged plastic beauty of by broken heart. i take another deep breath.

and i see how sometimes you don't let your shadow breathe because you haven't been plastic pretty in a while.

people talk about the love between the sun and the moon but no one talks about the way the sun loves the tiny star that limps around the moon known as the 'fault of the moon' that the sun dearly, dearly loves. and i wish people talked more about how beautiful and courageous it is to love someone's faults rather than their sculpted perfections

you're that one hand. that one hand that has marks for decorations on the base of the wrist, that one hand whose elbow bulges out because starvation became your friend for a while.

and your heart's a dull red because you crossed so many oceans for people who lied about their very destinations to you. you crossed oceans and fell on the sand, tired, broken, witnessing an emptiness no one ever warned you about. sometimes we promise too much when we hold too little to give. that is the worst thing you can do to someone.

Sparkle

i like the way you moved. it wasn't masculine or feminine, and that is what i loved about it the most i guess - it wasn't a stereotype - you aren't a stereotype

you are just unapologetically yourself, beyond labels and personality classifications. i didn't know people like that still existed.

your movements reminded me of purity, of unfiltered truth and the most bare fresh form of nature.

and then

then i fell in love with you

because how many people have you met - that love the sparkle just because its sparkle and not because it sparkles?

Kind Stranger

you're the most beautiful person i know. you don't remember how i like my coffee or my secret love for gardening. but you're something that my loved ones are not.

you're a kind stranger - and there's something about you

i could get drunk on the smell of your breath, your manner of wearing the dark brown suspenders and having ice cream with fingers. you look me in the eye like you know, and like its okay to be fragile. like its okay for me to be surprised upon finding a stranger - a stranger who's kind, a stranger who touches like feather and talks like wool. a stranger who wants good and talks of so much love and wellness. a stranger who smiles at you when you don't, who helps you pick up the bag you dropped when you struggled with your luggage with a tear stained face.

i'm sitting in the waiting room of the hospital and although its made in the way thats meant to block out the struggling heartbeats, like the colourful bouquet of flowers, the scented candles, the religious sculptures, the faded curtains and the shine of the sun - but the heartbeats find a way. the struggling heartbeats find a way to get to the waiting room and somewhere between 11 am and 12 pm i wish they find their way in the real sense too.

nothing's good and if there's something i've mastered that's my special pretentious aroma and sense of existence. i flip through the magazine but within i'm crumbling to bits, i'm curling to bits and there's no one to hold me from the inside. my husbands' arms around me on the outside do a little and i'm afraid - i'm afraid to look him in the eye and tell him that. and as i sit here in the waiting room full of struggling heartbeats i realise, i realise there are so many things that i am afraid of.

i hide a sniff and look across the room. a boy, mere 18 years old, stood near the window in a way that captured my interest a little. you know when someone just exists and it fascinates you? the aroma of their breath and the posture of their body, the curve of their hands and the colour of their clothes. there's a soft frown on his face and i could blame the struggling heartbeats for that but it looks like its more from the happy of the sun. i've never seen a happy frown in my life.

he looks at me, and smiles. the sides of his lips tilt upwards as if praying to the God for the betterment of this world and i think wow. i think i just got saved a little, i think there's a pair of arms holding me from within, creating a small brick wall between the struggling heartbeats and mine.

and i don't feel alone anymore. i feel there's another whisper of a voice praying with me, praying for the amelioration of this world, for the heartbeats to struggle a little less maybe or maybe the struggle to be a bit less struggling in itself.

i don't hide my next sob and hug my husband tighter. there's a happiness radiating off his chest as i place my ear next to his erratic heartbeat which pleads for some access.

i look across the room to that boy again and he's gone.

he's gone

but i don't think he'll ever really be.

Concert Love

our fingers brushed and it wasn't electricity but more or less like the elegant flame of a candle

the concert was banging loud and my ears were full of sloppy noises of kisses

couples making out

girls on top of guys or locked in embrace of them

something about them shouted 'we're away, so, so far away from the world'

his sweat mixed with mine and a flame took birth in the pit of my stomach

i got off the smell of our sweats together

and right amidst the loud crowd roaring and floating to the music of the concert

were us

we

"i feel like we're the centre of the world," his lips brailed on the surface of my ear i wanted to say we're not, we're not the centre of the world, but rather a small star living the anonymity amongst millions

my eyes spoke for me and when i looked at him,

he smiled like he knew

the buzz of the stage vibrated our hips together and i closed my eyes to think about our warm couch, burgundy and worn out, it has 4 holes, one of which i play them while we watch rerun of friends every weekend,

i was in love with him and where we were. where people look but don't stare, where you could be dirty and the others would smile, smile like they know, they know how fucking phenomenal dirty feels,

his wiry arms were wrapped around my waist and his hands didn't touch, he was much smaller than me but thats how exactly he could drop his head and get lost in the damp curve of my neck.

my neck could sniff the stale beer off his bare lips and i shivered in his hold, his arms didn't touch in front of my waist and i covered his small fingers with mine, feeling the leftover smitts of crisps and burnt out joints,

the anonymity we shared

i craved that to be known but ignored, thats like our concert love

he and i mumbled the lyrics in between

i don't doubt this at all

i want to take you everywhere i go

make a home that no one would know

like stars for lights and stale beer for water

each others' skin for food and your tongue for dessert

our bodies for blankets and my chest for bed

you for my breath and i for your obsession of words said

i want to take you everywhere i go

make a home that no one would know

take the train to venice and catch flights to places

like names we don't know and visiting places too entrancing to be real

and i know sometimes i'd wake up at three in the morning and cry a little

because i'll be looking at you and it'll feel like magic

the depth of your magic that cleaned my wounds with a clean cloth of love every night and shouted my name with a silent gasp every time i painted you with my come

i want to take you everywhere i go

make a home that no one would know

the degree of our embrace getting tighter with every word of the song we husked

"fuck"

i never ever wanna let go

the fireworks should've bolted us but they glued us tighter, his hands almost touching from around my waist and his lips dented in like a part of my skeleton, my bones moulding into his and this?

this was the best night of my life

and i want to tell him

instead, i say

i want to take you everywhere i go

make a home that no one would know

this is our concert love

and suddenly there's water everywhere from the hoses and there wouldn't be a more perfect moment

i turn around and we kiss oh so slow

the fireworks look like a mayhem of stars behind his head and i smile into the kiss

because he'll go everywhere i wish to take him, making a home that no one would know about

everywhere including places like this concert

and homes like this concert love that we share

i look at him with all i have and i can't think of words to tell him that its like we're already on that train to venice amidst bores of water and drops of stale beer, kissing breaths away and building new homes with our sweats together every single day

concert love,

this is our concert love

We

we talked right here. his face resembled a rose and i see not many colours but his eye shade was that of a rainbow and the ice cream we had felt too warm and the coffee too cold. it gave me goosebumps, and our first kiss, right here, reminded me of a galaxy thats yet to be discovered. a galaxy with stars that shine during the day.

your smile made me think that maybe rainbows have hundreds of colours and smiling through sadness is better than laughing loud. there is a series of photographs on the wall behind you and the frame of each is like capturing the different angles of your face. storing them as memories, like polaroids hanging off threads, polaroids you look at in the middle of the day, caressing it and you gulp tight because the memory lies so heavy and beautiful in your chest. you bite your lip and mumble nervous vowels and i laugh within because you - you are just so you. there's nothing else i can say about you. you are kind and gentle and all the great things in the world. you're soothing when there's a fire around me and the hand that holds me still when the world spins too fast. you're the edges making life simple and directions in a maze where i'm lost.

Deaths Are Not Okay

some silences stretch a little too long and we fail to notice

and there will always be some things i won't be able to forgive you for

you're buried in deep

an alternate universe where the globe might be square

sky green and ground a beautiful blue

but deaths are not okay

whining dogs never look happy and a cushion full of stones never a comfort

roses without thorns are not beautiful and let me tell you

it wasn't okay to die

you deserved to live

you deserved to smile once more and laugh another laugh with her right beside you

i wish i was that her

the epitome of perfection and the language of love for you

but i could only

only ever just wish

but deaths are not okay

you deserved to live

you deserved to get kissed once more and kiss more

you deserved to drive away to another city and lose yourself before losing yourself

and deaths?

some days

deaths are not okay

the lamp in your room refuses to work

the fan stays still

the white room is a dull black all of a sudden

and you

you deserved to live

i wish i had noticed your silence

Our Little Scarred World

it was dark and i looked at him long

    longer enough for a surprise of a stare

    and also because scars don't show in the dark

    he unzipped his pants, gentling down the base of his underwear

    the cease of his thighs was a milky white

    with a dark brown line

    i touched the molest and thought of my favourite milky way

    and i cried looking at his beautiful white shaded hair, eyes a light blue with even more lightness of tiredness and hands pale cold

    "we all have scars," he murmured - "in more ways than one,"

    i opened the buttons of my shirt

    my chest shook with pain and my heart pounded, screaming for help his suffering hands touched the uneven fixed skin on the base of my right rib and i thought where has he come from

"you're my first in more ways than one," i murmured right back

there we sat under my favourite tree with scars putting up a show of misery, with our hands caressing the breath of each others' suffering, under the half moon with stars singing the melody of my favourite song and my horse padding the lines from my favourite book.

and i thought if there wouldn't be a world better than this - our little scarred world.

Our Rivers

we're like this river right here

    like two inseparable graceful drops of water

    flowing together

    bright and blue

    in the rear view of those lovers holding hands

    we're this river that would never stop moving

    that would never be dead

    no matter the grim, the dirt, the ash

    vim and vigour of our breaths against each other

    kisses unseen amidst other water drops

    i drink you and you drink me

    the savoury victuals of our blue blood

    i

    drink you

and

you

you drink me

like the river that would never be dead

He Makes Me Pray

he makes me pray when i'm numb

   folding my hands

   making me reach out with a belief that there's a voice somewhere

   a voice in the form of a rainbow

   a piece of gold

   or lacklustre of a diamond

   its like hypnosis

   praying with him

   you're my hope for my first breath after death

Be Careful

and we stand beside the railing with blank eyes
    staring at tomorrows and blinking at yesterdays
    its raining and the sky sobs a little in between
    we pretend not to notice
    you hand me pearls
    like you'd handed me your heart a few years ago
    and whisper in my ears
    "be careful
    these are made out of my tears,"

Your Eyes

your eyes

    a misty blue

    spikes of cold ice

    snow storm

    an undiscovered sea

I Don't See You Anymore

i searched everywhere for you

on the road where we kissed and in the dairy i wrote about you every night

i saw you but i didn't at the same time

you smiled but you didn't and you laughed but you didn't

a piece in you has gone missing

and thats all i feel like now.

a small piece that doesn't belong

on the road where we kissed, you were the word gentle. you were soft hands and a warm embrace.

in the diary i wrote about you every night in, you were the word moon. a shining measure with a million thousand stories to tell.

but we grew up.

and a piece of you got lost, the road was forgotten and i can't find my diary anymore.

we grew up and the moon is a dull white for me, warmness is something i despise and i don't keep diaries anymore on some nights, i still search for you

in look alike dark alleys and old schools, doggy pubs and unknown bars but i can never find you

i search for that piece of you in playgrounds, roads that lead nowhere and highways that go beyond my boundary,

you're nowhere to be seen. you've grown up. you're not warm. you're not the moon.

i look at you. but i don't see you anymore.

Troublemakers

i had a dream where a man took a bullet for me

    he was called

    the troublemaker

    he wore black like a heavenly white

    and i was drawn

    i was drawn to his sincere mischief

    he was like a dandelion

    some chose to see him as a seed

    some chose to make a wish upon him

    watch his wings fly away with the wind

    there'll always be people who'd take bullets for you and yet you'd be oblivious to the sound of the gun triggering

    troublemakers - they are capable of love too

    black - it cannot be made without white

    dandelions is not just a flower - it carries wishes

Legs

there was something about her legs

they weren't lean, or long, or curvy,

she had freckles near her knees and wounds on her feet

no pair of heels would fit her and on Saturday nights she'd come home all swollen

she'd sleep on the couch thereafter, with drool sliding down her chin

murmuring nothings in her sleep about how tired she is, but how the show was a blast

i'd take her legs in my lap and she wouldn't flinch a bit

i fit my fingers in the gaps between her toes and wiggle them

pressing the nail of every toe, scalping the skin of her ankle, caressing the skin of her calf and the back of her knees, discovering new wounds i reckon she'd tell me about the morning after

i'd hug her legs and go to sleep

only to be woken up in the middle of the night by a sleepy sniff of happiness opening my eyes, i'd look at her feet, snuggled in my stomach, my hands around her knees, and her sleepy eyes staring right at me

i'd stare back and smile a moment later

we forgot to have dinner together but right now i feel that its okay

its okay we don't get time like other couples to go out, to have sex every day and click thousands of pictures

right now, as she smiles back at me, it feels okay

slowly, seconds turn into minutes and the staring game reaches a soft end as both of us doze off for the second time that very night.

she's my *her*

always

I'll Always Dream of You

my dead friend - he visits me on weekends when i can't sleep. i lie awake, alert - waiting, on the bed. a pillow perched beside me to welcome him. he shows up between 12 to 2 am. sometimes even after 2. i mean to ask him one day, what makes him be so late, but i decide off it.

you're staring at yourself in the mirror

a voice comes beside me. he adjusts himself on the bed, shoulder to shoulder we shit. i don't chance a look at him.

one sided love is painful - even here, in the blurred line between death and life. between him and me.

been thinking

i murmur. he holds my hand and i close my eyes. hours pass and the sensation of his palm on mine never goes away. every thought from my mind suddenly slides down a sparkling rainbow and i'm in water. i love water. i've always loved water. i look to my right, my dead friend smiles at me and back floats. he's shining and the water, with sun, reflect off another rainbow from his skin. he's like existing magic and a cup of tea that never runs cold. he goes under water and i follow him, like i always have.

and suddenly its dark again. but its good dark. calm dark.

its a bright dark.

my lashes flutter as i open them to see the pretentious sun outside my window smile at me. i think of the big hole in my chest - i think of water, rainbow - and a dead friend.

i dream of you. i'll always dream of you.

Conversations

the conversations we have go beyond you and i. they go beyond we and us. this world and this universe. they go beyond the concept of humanity and practicality.

the visual of our conversations would be my nails scratching your chest with peels of your skin coming off, it would be you licking the hidden hollow of my ear that i'm almost always too afraid to show. they're a thunderstorm, an uninvited, abrupt, scary, and bold, thunderstorm.

its like internal fucking, the conversations we have. fucking of hearts and lungs and our systems. its the fucking we can't control and don't even wish to.

we look at each other when we talk and there's this electricity that strikes, warmer than the summer we fell in love and sharper than the spikes of ice from our first winter together. but at the same time, its melted fruits too, its devoured melted fruits and your first swim without floaters in a river full of life beneath you. its that tingling sensation of being licked and bitten by your loved one in the morning and silent exchanging of breaths instead of a kiss as a goodnight. our conversations, they are things people don't get anymore, they are things that sometimes some poets end up writing about. they are our things - always.

Hands

two five year old boys stare up at the sky and mumble

i see a hand

they look at each other and giggle. the 8 year old, skinny, with a mushroom cut and red shorts points at the sky like its where they both belong. the 9 year old with suspenders and matching red shorts looks at the shy but ends up looking at the pointing hand of his friend. tan skin, freckles on his knuckles and a small daisy in between the gap of his forefinger and thumb. he smiles, thinking, that hand could be his sky.

he brings up his hand to the 8 year old's and matches them both palm palm.

ten tiny little fingers and a single pair of hands, two souls full of big hearts pumping for promises made over sand and dust to each other

hands - the 8 year old whispers

hands - the 9 year old whispers back, pushing his fingers in the spaces between and clutching their hands together

hands.

Kiss Me

kiss me, i really need you to kiss me
    looking at me in all ways that you can
    with candles near you and me in your bed
    with your mouth and eyes and your rough hands
    kiss me the way no one does anymore
    kiss me with your eyes open

Keep Writing

keep writing your story
    and i promise you
    one day
    it will hurt less